THE CAMPFIRE COLLECTION

GHOSTS, BEASTS, AND THINGS THAT GO BUMP IN THE NIGHT

THE CAMPFIRE COLLECTION

GHOSTS, BEASTS, AND THINGS THAT GO BUMP IN THE NIGHT

Edited by Kit Duane

CHRONICLE BOOKS
SAN FRANCISCO

Library of Congress Cataloging-in-
Publication Data available.

ISBN: 0-8118-3777-7

Manufactured in the United States
of America

Book and cover design by Public

Distributed in Canada by Raincoast Books
9050 Shaughnessy Street
Vancouver, British Columbia V6P 6E5

10 9 8 7 6 5 4 3 2 1

Chronicle Books LLC
85 Second Street
San Francisco, California 94105

www.chroniclebooks.com

THIS BOOK IS DEDICATED TO A GHOST

(OR FIGMENT OF MY IMAGINATION):

A spectral sheepherder, who
With a hungry-looking dog
Wanders the hills of a vast sheep
ranch south of Coalinga, California.

INTRODUCTION 8

MOUNTAINS

Ice Sculptures *13*
David B. Silva

Creature of the Snows *27*
William Sambrot

BEACH

Xenos Beach *43*
Graham Joyce

FOREST

Death to the Easter Bunny *65*
Alan Ryan

We Have Always Lived in the Forest *91*
Nancy Holder

Prologue: As the Wolf Loves Winter *104*
David Poyer

Caught in the Jaws of Death *114*
Jerry MacDonald

SWAMP

Survival Exercise *125*
Talmage Powell

Swamp Horror *142*
Will Smith and R. J. Robbins

PLAINS

The Valley of the Spiders *157*
H. G. Wells

Waziah *172*
Joe R. Lansdale

The Spectre Bride *193*
Anonymous

FARM

Bloody Polly *199*
Michael Norman and Beth Scott

The Faceless Thing *206*
Edward D. Hoch

EXOTIC

Allal *215*
Paul Bowles

The Quest for Blank Claveringi *230*
Patricia Highsmith

BIOGRAPHIES *250*
ACKNOWLEDGMENTS *255*

INTRODUCTION

The stories in this collection are best read around a forest camp-fire or in a lonely country cabin. A tent site in the mountains near looming stones will work, as will one in the desert when the moon is full and coyotes are howling. Most importantly, though, read these stories out loud and in company because terrifying stories become, strangely enough, bonds of exhilaration and shared experience.

The frightening stories in this collection do not belong to the "atrocity genre." Rather they conjure up a fear of the unknown that can become especially acute in the wild. Most wilderness "ghost" stories are the tales of beasts. Some of these beasts are changelings, in the tradition of werewolves, and they have a dark agenda when it comes to human beings. Some are the frightening remnants of a humanoid race; some are dark, amoeba-like forms from the primordial ooze. A very few tales describe transcendent creatures, living in a primitive Eden. The oldest stories of humankind concern unearthly beings walking the face of the earth, beings who can't be understood and who capriciously destroy lives. If we choose to listen to our fears and the stories they tell, there's nothing like doing so on a luminous, otherworldly night, when we can't help but throw another log on the fire and move closer to our friends in the flickering light.

I'll never forget an evening when tales of the super-natural brought a group of friends together in a sort of rapturous terror and excitement. We were staying in a mountain cabin and finishing dinner around a beat-up log table when someone began telling a ghost story—about a gold miner killed by his partner during the California gold rush, in the foothills near the cabin. Local people, the storyteller told us, reported that the miner's ghost still wandered the trails, looking for the man who'd done him in. Sometimes, thinking he'd found him, the spectral miner hunted down an innocent hiker. Examining the bruised body, he'd realize he'd made a mistake and vow never again to attempt revenge. But every twenty years or so, desire so overpowered him that he made another attempt. In fact, it was just twenty years ago this weekend, said the storyteller, that the ghost miner had made his last mistake. And in the morning, all of us around that table were taking off on a backpacking trip!

We drew closer, laughing nervously. We were friends from the city; we'd gone to business meetings together and to the same dinner parties. Some of us played on an amateur soccer team together. We were good conversationalists, yet I don't believe any one of us had ever told the other a ghost story. That night, we each had a tale to tell, whether it was a ghost story or an extrasensory experience. Our tales had had a life of their own, were waiting in our heads and wanted outing. As we told our stories, we kept glancing over at the un-curtained windows and at the flickering candles, as if they were forces to be reckoned with. We spoke of telepathy, of silent running dogs who appeared in nightmares as harbingers of disaster, and of the wandering spirit of a black bear shaman, known to wait on trails for a lone woman hiker to pass by. If he caught her eye, he turned her into a bear, and she spent the rest of her life haunting campground dumpsters, grubbing for human food.

The night in the cabin became the story of a group of friends—how they sat with each other in the candlelight on a dark night becoming more and more frightened, and how, when a cell phone rang, three people leapt up, knocking over their chairs, and another screamed. Then we all burst out laughing, partly out of relief, but mostly because scaring ourselves was fun. Possibly, an evening around the campfire telling these stories will produce the same bonding experience between you and your friends as storytelling did for us. We all wanted that bonding experience, of course, but as the spectral miner said to the backpacker hiking alone on the trail: Be careful what you wish for. You might get it.

Good luck!
—Kit Duane

ICE SCULPTURES

David B. Silva

I thought I'd forgotten.

Spring, summer, and autumn have each since come and gone, and I guess it was easy to fool myself into believing the past was finally something left to cold impossible yesterdays. Out of season, out of mind. But things unfinished have a way of hovering around the edges of your life until you can't ignore them any longer. I guess that's why I had to get the film developed. I guess that's why I'm not surprised by the photograph I always knew would be there.

Yesterdays never really let go of your soul. They just pretend they've gone away until they're ready to return again . . .

Eagle Peak in the summertime was a soft white cloud hanging mid-universe somewhere between heaven and earth. Swallow up the air, it would chill your soul. Cup your hands and sip the water from its lake, it would remind you how alive you really were. Each breath was the incense of fresh cut pine, each glance a bright and bountiful rainbow of alpine flowers.

It's that summer aliveness I've tried to remember about Eagle Peak. But it's the winter I can't seem to forget.

It's such a cold queer season, winter is. Of dark dreams and hibernations. Of snow that floats gently from heaven-to-earth like white milky butterflies, so deceivingly turning marrow to ice, summer to a vague memory. Spellbinding. Let it once lull you to sleep, it'll take you to death. Touch its tapered icicles— hanging stalactite-like from tree and rock, sometimes dripping, sometimes not—and before you're aware, the pellucid ice turns red with your blood.

Mother Nature at her wickedest, is winter.

Mother Nature at her wickedest.

When we first established camp at Eagle Peak, it was late in the summer of '80, a year that had no autumn. One September day was all blue skies and T-shirts, the next was gray gloom and parkas. That same year, in fact only a few months before, Mount St. Helens had explosively erupted, sending a plume of ash as high as fifteen miles into the atmosphere. And meteorologists were already warning that the ash might have a significant influence on weather patterns. Something like a small Nuclear Winter, they were forecasting for some parts of the country.

But who listens to meteorologists?

Stairway To Heaven is what we called our little commune at Eagle Peak. A little esoteric and self-copulating of us, but that's the way of the artist. A government grant brought us together. Something about interpreting the four seasons through different artistic mediums. (Unfortunately, it wasn't Frankie Valli and The Four Seasons. At the time, my perspective on music was much better formulated than my perspective on falling leaves or cold spring showers.) It was a nebulous undertaking at best, but as long as the government was willing to flip the bill, I, and others, were willing to follow along.

We located our little Stairway in a small valley—a cliff of rock to the north to protect us from the northerners that sometimes swept through the park, and an open lane to the south where we hoped the southern sun would keep us warm on those cold January days when the skies were cloudless.

There were twelve of us, all previous strangers, all on separate paths of artistic endeavor—wood carving, leathercraft, oils, sculpting, acting, photography, etc. I was the Hemingway of the group. As much as possible, we were each supposed to integrate the resources of nature into our work. Paints were made from berries and saps and chalk-like rocks, leather from animal hides, wood carved fresh from fallen trees, etc.

Creativity run rampant, you could say.

As the lone writer, I suspect my presence at the Stairway was more for the purpose of recording the experience than anything else. The grant wasn't terribly explicit about expected outcomes. But for my own vague intentions (which have long since been abandoned), I had high hopes of compiling a book of the folklore and mystique that I thought might eventually come to play a part in our back-to-nature experience.

I guess I gave up those intentions when I was no longer able to comprehend exactly what was taking place at the Stairway.

There were two of us who matched up as outsiders right from day one. Margo McKennen was a photographer, full of f-stops and shutter-speeds, wide-angles and zooms. In a way, we were each observer more than creator, and sometimes I think that fine distinction was what kept us a cold breath apart from the others. On the artistic social ladder, Margo and I each had one foot on the bottom rung and one foot dangling free. I think there must have been an unwritten rule (naturally it would have been unwritten) about the dirtier the hands in the creation of one's art, the higher up the ladder one stood. Margo and I, we were just doing our best to keep aboard.

When I first met Margo, her camera was always busy whirr-clicking this and that with a nervous energy that never seemed satisfied. In some ways, I imagined that camera as an extension of her. She saw the world—for all its ugliness, and all its splendor—through an open shutter, almost as if she were afraid to put the camera down for fear she might miss something that shouldn't be missed. "Blink once, and a piece of the world goes scampering by unnoticed," she would say. "Blink twice . . . and there's nothing left to see."

When she first pulled that line on me, I thought it had something to do with being one of life's non-participators. But now, when I think back to the sadness that sometimes darkened her eyes at such times, I wonder if perhaps it was the blindness of death she was warning me about.

Blink twice . . . and there's nothing left to see.

It was September 16th when the first snowflake came fluttering down from the heavens, melting against the ground of Eagle Peak. Then another flake came whispering out of the sky, and another, and it was only a short time before they quit melting as they kissed the earth.

Two days later, a park ranger—all yellow-jacketed and puffing out great breaths of hot air—came snow-mobiling up the trail. They were closing the park (something usually reserved for after the Thanksgiving weekend), and he wanted to know if there were any . . . "last requests" is how he put it. I remember how he was trying his best to keep warm, clapping his hands together and scratching at the snow like a great elk trying to uncover the skeleton of a snow-hidden shrub. And beneath his words, there was a poorly-hidden tone. *Goddamn fools!* he was saying. *This ain't no place to be. Not this winter. Not here.*

They officially closed the park on September 20th, 1980.

And that began the longest winter I've ever experienced.

During those first winter days, Margo and I were detached observers, more or less keeping a wide eye on our fellow artists, and a curious eye on the strange weather. She was fascinated with the bitter cold of the early snow storm. And I guess that's what I found so attractive about her, that wonderful child-like curiosity, always wanting to poke a finger here or there and wait to see what happened.

Together—for we became almost inseparable after a while—we watched as our artistic cohorts slowly lost their facelessness and became real people, whole and eccentric and Jekyll-and-Hyde-ish each in some personal way. It was during those early winter days, when Margo and I were standing just at the fringe of the Stairway experience, left alone to take our little notes—both visual and written—that I enjoyed the most.

Of the lot, Billy Dayton, our resident sculptor, was the oddest. He was a man out of his time, a lost child of the sixties. He wore his hair long, tied in a ponytail with a strap of fur taken from a rabbit. His face was hidden behind a full beard with touches of gray that made him look older than his age. And his eyes were as dark as a moonless night.

I met him one late-summer day about a mile from camp. He was kneeling at the base of a monolithic slab of volcanic rock, chipping at it with a chisel made of granite.

"What is it?" I asked, in all innocence of the answer.

"The revolution of nature," he answered with a voice soft and fragile, and the kind of voice that makes you believe every muttered syllable even though you know it's nonsense. And that was Billy Dayton, always talking nonsense and making it sound right. At least that's the way I saw it at the time. Now . . . well, now I'm not so sure. Perhaps it wasn't nonsense at all.

"Catchy title," I said.

Then Margo came along, *whirr-clicking* away at everything that found its way into her camera frame. When she saw Billy's monolith, she snapped off four or five shots, then paused with her camera clutched in her hands. "What is it?" she asked.

"The revolution of nature," I answered.

She didn't giggle, at least not out loud.

But something hit Dayton wrong, because he turned on his knees and caught eyes with her, as if he were reading her mind. I remember for just a moment, thinking his eyes were afire with liquid mercury. Then Margo shivered, and I could see the joy shrivelling up inside of her, the way a child's joy sometimes shrivels when an adult walks into the room.

"Let's go," she said, giving my arm a tug. Her hand was ice-cold, as if the blood had drained out of her body.

I followed along, while Billy turned back to his *revolution*. And when we were out of ear shot, I asked Margo why the sudden escape.

"Just a feeling," she said. Then her camera came up and she was *whirr-clicking* first this tree, then that one. And that was the first time I realized Margo's camera wasn't just a window to the world, but was also her way of closing off the things she didn't want to see.

Out of frame, out of mind.

As winter nights grew colder, the Stairway slowly divided into smaller and smaller groups, each with its own self-interest. Inside this tent, a great debate on craft versus art, and which is the soul of creativity. Inside that tent, a sharing of berry-paint recipes and ten great uses for volcanic rock. Inside our tent, Margo and I—once strangers, now friends—safely shared tiny, protected pieces of ourselves.

"Perspective is the greatest gift we can give the world," she said on one of those cold nights. She was bundled warmly in a mummy bag, the flickering light of the fire reflecting brightly in her eyes. "Outside, you see the bleakness of a harsh winter, I see ice castles and snow fairies. We look at the same thing, yet see it differently. That perspective—yours unique to you, mine unique to me—is our greatest gift to the world."

I thought I could understand that. "Take the same idea for a story," I said. "Give it to fifty different writers and you'll get fifty different stories. Each with its own personality.

Each as individual as its writer."

"Yes!" she shouted excitedly, teacher to student. "And from where do we draw our unique perspectives, you yours, me mine?"

"From yesterdays and todays! From childhood delights and adolescent nightmares! From staring monkey-like at the mirror! From growing up so fast we never quit feeling like we're still children!"

"And from the smells we smell!" she said, raising up on one elbow and spitting out the words as fast as they'd come. "And the sounds we hear, the roughs and smooths and squares and rounds we touch! From what makes us sad, and what makes us happy! From our beliefs about the world and the universe, about birth and death, about promises and lies! From all of it!"

And she took up a great breath, held it, smiled through it, then let it all out in a white cloud that filled up the tent. And she had said so much more than she realized at that moment. Because I think that's what happened to Dayton. He had a perspective all his own, and somehow it got loose.

"I want you to see this," she told me one late-January day. The sun was shining free over Eagle Peak and the white snow was nearly blinding as she tugged at me. "It's beauty at its ugliest."

"That's a contradiction in terms. It must have something to do with Dayton," I said.

"Who else?"

"Another revolution?"

"Of sorts, I suppose." She stopped to snap off a few quick pictures of some deer tracks in the snow. "Take a guess at what the man has done this time. Make it the wildest, most bizarre guess you can come up with."

"He's built his own stairway to heaven," I said.

Margo lowered her camera, then shared the oddest smile with me, as if she were giving actual thought to the possibility. "I wonder," she said softly. Then the camera went up again, and she said, "Guess again."

"I give up. The man's too unpredictable for a writer's imagination."

"He's sculpting in ice."

"Sculpting what?"

"A self-portrait."

There were three sculptures cut in the ice, each slightly different in a not-so-subtle way I still find difficult to describe. A progression of some sort—young, old, older, first came to mind. The first, a marvelous likeness of Dayton himself. The second, a little less recognizable. The third, Picasso-like, only softer, less sharp in line and cut. Perhaps *digression* might better describe the three since each appeared less distinct, more oblique than the one to its left.

"That's a self-portrait?" I asked. There was an odd sense of *imbalance* about the work, something that seemed to say: *the wiser the man, the more self-destructive.* And that was Dayton himself, wise and self-destructive.

"What else can it be?" Margo answered.

* * *

Dayton damned all twelve of us that winter, we each became one of his ice-cut similitudes done in three distinct digressions—born, living, dead—as if the breath of death had slowly shriveled the ice. All twelve of us, he cut and shaped and sculpted. Sally at 7,000 feet, near Eagle Lake. Hampton at 7,500 feet near Goat Head Pass. The others hidden in places we were never able to locate.

At the completion of the last sculptured likeness, sometime in mid-April when the snow at the lower elevations was already beginning to turn to water, Dayton disappeared inside his tent and never came out again.

We didn't know it at the time, but the "revolution" was on its way.

It arrived near the end of April. The sun was shining almost summer-like in the southern skies. And the spring thaw was slowly lending life to an endless number of trickles and runnels and fountains, sculpting deeper into mountainsides, and here and there rearranging the topographical anatomy.

Eagle's Peak was finally coming back to life after its long winter hibernation. And I for one could hardly wait for the day when I could let out a warm sigh and not see it mushrooming before me in the cold air.

And as much as I thought of myself as nature's victim, I suspect Dayton thought of himself as nature's messiah. And perhaps that's what he was—Mother Nature's messenger. It had been two weeks since anyone had seen him poke his nose outside his tent flaps, so Margo—her wondrous curiosity piqued—convinced me we should try poking our noses inside for a glimpse.

"This isn't the time to be taking photographs,"

I whispered to her. We were standing outside Dayton's tent, Margo with both hands on her camera, me with both hands on the canvas flaps.

"Just one," she said with a sparkle in her eye. "Go on."

And I pulled back the flaps.

And Margo snapped off two or three quick shots.

And we both stood silent for the longest breath, Margo's camera dropping numbly back to her side (a sight I'll never forget, because it was the first time I had ever seen her come face-to-face with something horrible and not try to hide herself behind the lens of a camera).

What was left of Dayton was on the floor, partially hidden beneath some clothing and that strap of rabbit fur he always used to tie back his hair. I nudged a foot against the pile, heard the eerie clicking of bone-against-bone, saw the jelly-like substance ooze outward a little further, and tried to keep my stomach from heaving.

Dayton-the-messiah had delivered his message.

Something in Mother Nature was out of balance.

Stairway To Heaven disbanded the next day, partly because of what had happened to Dayton, in part because the long winter months had finally taken their toll on our collective state of mind. Even in the face of spring, it had become too easy to see things as forever cold and frozen and hopeless.

Sally and Hampton left early the next morning for Mount St. Helens. Some of the others went home, some went south where the weather was warmer, some drifted out of camp without saying. Margo and I stayed on.

We were curious, I guess. And maybe that's what had set us apart from the others right from the beginning. I think Margo felt somehow responsible for what had happened to Dayton, though we both tried to label it as a fluke of nature, something like spontaneous combustion, something better left unquestioned. Still, she wanted to keep taking photographs until (through the eyes of her camera) it somehow made sense. And for myself, well, I wanted to write more about Dayton and how he seemed so different from the rest of us, and maybe how things at the Stairway might have been different if we'd tried to understand him a little better.

We both felt compelled to remain at Eagle Peak a little longer.

The twenty-first day of May was my last day there.

I was sitting on the ground, leaning back against a rock, soaking up some sunshine, and scribbling stray ideas into my notebook. I couldn't escape the thought that somehow Dayton and Mount St. Helens and the ice sculptures were all intertwined in some strange malevolent way that had brought about Dayton's death.

Then Margo quietly appeared from the mouth of a small valley that fed into a single-file trail leading upward toward Eagle Peak's 12,000 foot summit. Her camera was resting at her side. Her steps were nearly staggering, and I remember my first thought being that she must have tried to hike to the top of the mountain. She was glistening in the mid-day sun, her hair was damp against her forehead, her face and arms and legs were alive with reflected sunlight. And her eyes were glassy and ice-like, as pure as the crystal-like agates I used to play marbles with as a child.

"Margo?" I had her rest against the rock, knelt next to her, and noticed for the first time the blood coming from her head. "My God, what happened?"

She handed me a roll of film—the touch of her hand was cold, like a mountain stream in early May—then another, and another. And when she tried to smile it was a sad smile she couldn't hold. "You're still up there," she whispered. "I couldn't reach you, but you're there."

I brushed the hair away from where she was bleeding, there was a dark red hole where her left ear should have been. "Oh, Margo."

"I found my ice sculpture," she said, between a number of small, fought-for breaths. "Thought maybe if I shattered it . . ."

"Dayton's likeness of you?"

She nodded. "Yours, too. Another thousand feet up. Near the summit."

There was a long, breath-held silence. I sat next to her then, she curled herself into my arms. "I'm dying," she said, and it was as innocent and honest a statement as one of her photographs. "And there's nothing I can do."

She leaned into me. I whispered, "I love you," and pulled her closer. She felt soft, too soft, like a worn pillow or a balloon losing its air. Her skin was moist and cold and slick to the touch, wax-like in some ways, ice-like in others. And I knew I was going to lose her.

I held her till the sun went down, till I couldn't see in the darkness any longer, because I wanted to remember what she looked like before the flesh began sliding off her arms and legs and face, before the tissue and muscle and cartilage turned jelly-like and puddled beneath her. And when there was only a distant, hazy moonlight overhead, I listened to the final clattering of her bones, and felt the last of her form melt beneath our embrace the way the last of her ice sculpture was melting beneath the May sky two thousand feet higher up the mountain . . .

It's raining outside.

I've left the windows open and the heat off and still I can't help feeling too hot on this winter day. I know what's happening to me, though that doesn't make it any less painful, any less hideous.

In the photograph, taken from a distance, I can see where my ice-sculptured likeness is sitting proud just a few hundred feet below the Eagle Peak summit. Low enough to be warmed by three seasons of sun, high enough to somehow resist the melting. And I feel like an icicle in the late afternoon of an overcast day, moist to the touch, dripping here and there just a bit, but ever so grateful for the first chill of the coming cold night.

CREATURE OF THE SNOWS

CREATURE OF THE SNOWS

William Sambrot

Ed McKale straightened up under his load of cameras and equipment, squinting against the blasting wind, peering, staring, sweeping the jagged, unending expanse of snow and wind-scoured rock. Looking, searching, as he'd been doing now for two months, cameras at the ready.

Nothing. Nothing but the towering Himalayas, thrusting miles high on all sides, stretching in awesome grandeur from horizon to horizon, each pinnacle tipped with immense banners of snow plumes, streaming out in the wind, vivid against the darkly blue sky. The vista was one of surpassing beauty. Viewing it, Ed automatically thought of light settings, focal length, color filters—then just as automatically rejected the thought. He was here on top of the world to photograph something infinitely more newsworthy, if only he could find it.

The expedition paused, strung out along a ridge of blue snow, with shadows falling away to the right and left into terrifying abysses, and Ed sucked for air. Twenty thousand feet is really quite high, although many of the peaks beyond rose nearly ten thousand feet above him.

Up ahead, the Sherpa porters (each a marvelous shot—gap-toothed, ebullient grins, seamed faces, leathery brown) bowed under stupendous loads for this altitude, leaning on their coolie crutches, waiting for Dr. Schenk to make up his mind. Schenk, the expedition leader, was arguing with the guides again, his breath spurting little puffs of vapor, waving his arms, pointing down.

Obviously Schenk was calling it quits. He was within his rights, Ed knew; two months was all Schenk had contracted for. Two months of probing snow and ice; scrambling over crevasses, up rotten rock cliffs, wind-ravaged, bleak, stretching endlessly toward Tibet and the never-never lands beyond. Two months of searching for footprints where none should be. Searching for odors, for droppings, anything to disclose the presence of creatures other than themselves. Without success.

Two months of nothing. Big, fat nothing.

The expedition was a bust. The goofiest assignment of this or any other century, as Ed felt it would be from the moment he'd sat across the desk from the big boss in the picture magazine's New York office two months ago, looking at a blurred photograph, while the boss filled him in on the weird details.

The photograph, his boss had told him gravely, had been taken in the Himalayan mountains, at an altitude of twenty-one thousand feet, by a man who had been soaring overhead in a motorless glider.

"A glider," Ed had said noncommittally, staring at the fuzzy, enlarged snapshot of a great expanse of snow and rocky ledges, full of harsh light and shadows, a sort of roughly bowl-shaped plateau apparently, and in the middle of it, a group of indistinct figures, tiny, lost against the immensity of great ice pinnacles. Ed looked closer. Were the figures people? If so, what had happened to their clothes?

"A glider," his boss reiterated firmly. The glider pilot, the boss said, was maneuvering in an updraft, attempting to do the incredible—soar over Mount Everest in a homemade glider. The wide-winged glider had been unable to achieve the flight over Everest, but flitting silently about seeking updrafts, it cleared a jagged pinnacle and there, less than a thousand feet below, the pilot saw movement where none should have been. And dropping lower, startled, he'd seen, the boss said dryly, "Creatures—creatures that looked exactly like a group of naked men and women and kids playing in the snow—at an altitude of twenty thousand five hundred feet." He'd had the presence of mind to take a few hasty snapshots before the group disappeared. Only one of the pictures had developed.

Looking at the snapshot with professional scorn, Ed had said, "These things are indistinct. I think he's selling you a bill of goods."

"No," the boss said, "we checked on the guy. He really did make the glider flight. We've had experts go over that blowup. The picture's genuine. Those are naked, biped, erect-walking creatures." He flipped the picture irritably. "I can't publish this thing. I want close-ups, action shots, the sort of thing our subscribers have come to expect of us."

He'd lighted a cigar slowly. "Bring me back some pictures I can publish, Ed, and you can write your own ticket."

"You're asking me to climb Mount Everest," Ed said carefully, keeping the sarcasm out of his voice, "to search for this plateau here," he tapped the shoddy photograph, "and take pix of—what are they—biped, erect-walking creatures, you say?"

The boss cleared his throat. "Not Mount Everest, Ed. It's Gauri Sankar, one of the peaks near Mount Everest. Roughly, it's only about twenty-three thousand feet or so high."

"That's pretty rough," Ed said.

The boss looked pained. "Actually it's not Gauri Sankar either. Just one of the lesser peaks of the Gauri Sankar massif. Well under twenty-three thousand. Certainly nothing to bother a hot-shot ex-paratrooper like you, Ed."

Ed winced, and the boss continued: "This guy—this glider pilot—wasn't able to pinpoint the spot, but he did come up with a pretty fair map of the terrain, for a pretty fair price. We've checked it out with the American Alpine Club; it conforms well with their own charts of the general area. Several expeditions have been in the vicinity but not at this exact spot, they tell me. It's not a piece of cake by any means, but it's far from being another Annapurna or K2 for accessibility."

He sucked at his cigar thoughtfully. "The Alpine Club says we've got only about two months of good weather before the inevitable monsoons hit that area, so time, as they say, is of the essence, Ed. But two months for this kind of thing ought to be plenty. Everything will be first class—we're even including these new gas guns that shoot hypodermic needles or something similar. We'll fly the essentials in to Katmandu and airdrop everything possible along the route up to your base,"—he squinted at a map—"Namche Bazar, a Sherpa village which is twelve thousand feet high."

He smiled amiably at Ed. "That's a couple of weeks march up from the nearest railhead and ought to get you acclimatized nicely. Plenty of experienced porters at Namche, all Sherpas. We've lined up a couple of expert mountain climbers with Himalayan backgrounds. And expedition leader will be Dr. Schenk, top man in his field."

"What is his field?" Ed asked gloomily.

"Zoology. Whatever these things are in this picture, they're animal, which is his field. Everyone will be sworn to secrecy. You'll be the only one permitted to use a camera, Ed. This could be the biggest thing you'll ever cover, if these things are what I think they are."

"What do you think they are?"

"An unknown species of man—or sub-man," his boss said, and prudently Ed remained silent. Two months would tell the tale.

But two months didn't tell.

Oh, there were plenty of wild rumors by the Nepalese all along the upper route. Hushed stories of the two-legged creature that walked like a man. A monster the Sherpas called Yeti. Legends. Strange encounters; drums sounding from snow-swept heights; wild snatches of song drifting down from peaks that were inaccessible to ordinary men. And one concrete fact: a ban, laid on by the Buddhist monks, against the taking of any life in the high Himalayas. What life? Ed wondered.

Stories, legends—but nothing else.

Two months of it. Starting from the tropical flatlands, up through the lush, exotic rain forest, where sun struggled through immense trees festooned with orchids. Two months, moving up into the arid foothills, where foliage abruptly ceased, and the rocks and wind took over. Up and ever up to where the first heavy snow pack lay. And higher still, following the trail laid out by the glider pilot. (And what impelled a man, Ed wondered, to soar over Mount Everest in a homemade glider?)

Two months during which Ed had come to dislike Dr. Schenk intensely. Tall, saturnine, smelling strongly of formaldehyde, Schenk classified everything into terms of vertebrate, invertebrate.

So now, standing on this wind-scoured ridge with the shadows falling into the abysses on either side, Ed peered through ice-encrusted goggles, watching Schenk arguing with the guides. He motioned to the ledge above, and obediently the Sherpas moved toward it. Obviously that would be the final camping spot. The two months were over by several days; Schenk was within his rights to call it quits. It was only Ed's assurances that the plateau they were seeking lay just ahead that had kept Schenk from bowing out exactly on the appointed time—that and the burning desire to secure his niche in zoology forever with a new specimen: biped, erect-walking—what?

But the plateau just ahead and the one after that and all the rest beyond had proved just as empty as those behind.

A bust. Whatever the unknown creatures were the

glider pilot had photographed, they would remain just that—unknown.

And yet as Ed slogged slowly up toward where the porters were setting up the bright blue and yellow nylon tents, he was nagged by a feeling that the odd-shaped pinnacle ahead looked awfully much like the one in the blurred photograph. With his unfailing memory for pictures, Ed remembered the tall, jagged cone that had cast a black shadow across a snowy plateau, pointing directly toward the little group that was in the center of the picture.

But Schenk wasn't having any more plateaus. He shook his head vehemently, white-daubed lips a grim line on his sun-blistered face. "Last camp, Ed," he said firmly. "We agreed this would be the final plateau. I'm already a week behind schedule. If the monsoons hit us, we could be in serious trouble below. We have to get started back. I know exactly how you feel, but I'm afraid this is it."

Later that night, while the wind moved ceaselessly, sucking at the tent, they burrowed in sleeping bags, talking.

"There must be some basis of fact in those stories," Ed said to Dr. Schenk. "I've given them a lot of thought. Has it occurred to you that every one of the sightings, the few face-to-face meetings of the natives and these, these unknowns, has generally been just around dawn and usually when the native was alone?"

Schenk smiled dubiously. "Whatever this creature may be—and I'm convinced that it's either a species of large bear or one of the great anthropoids—it certainly must keep off the well-traveled routes. There are very few passes through these peaks, of course, and it would be quite simple for them to avoid these locales."

"But we're not on any known trail," Ed said thoughtfully. "I believe our methods have been all wrong, stringing out a bunch of men, looking for trails in the snow. All we've done is announce our presence to anything with ears for miles around. That glider pilot made no sound; he came on them without warning."

Ed looked intently at Schenk. "I'd like to try that peak up ahead and the plateau beyond." When Schenk uttered a protesting cry, Ed said, "Wait—this time I'll go alone with just one Sherpa guide. We could leave several hours before day-break. No equipment, other than oxygen, food for one meal—and my cameras, of course. Maintain a strict silence. We could be back before noon. Will you wait long enough for this one last try?" Schenk hesitated. "Only a few hours more," Ed urged.

Schenk stared at him; then he nodded slowly. "Agreed. But aren't you forgetting the most important item of all?" When Ed looked blank, Schenk smiled. "The gas gun. If you should run across one, we'll need more proof than just your word for it."

There was a very little wind, no moon, but cold, the cold approaching that of outer space, as Ed and one Sherpa porter started away from the sleeping camp, up the shattered floor of an ice river that swept down from the jagged peak ahead.

They moved up, hearing only the squeak of equipment, the peculiar gritty sound of crampons biting into packed snow, an occasional hollow crash of falling ice blocks. To the east a faint line of gray was already visible; daylight was hours away, but at this tremendous height sunrise came early. They moved slowly, breathing through woolen masks, the thin air cutting cruelly into their lungs, moving up, up.

They stopped once for hot chocolate from a thermos, and Ed slapped the Sherpa's shoulder, grinning, pointing ahead to where the jagged peak glowed pink and gold in the first slanting rays of the sun. The Sherpa looked at the peak and quickly shifted his glance to the sky. He gave a long, careful look at the gathering clouds in the east, then muttered something, shaking his head, pointing back, back down to where the camp was hidden in the inky shadows of enormous boulders.

When Ed resumed the climb, the Sherpa removed the long nylon line which had joined them. The route was comparatively level, on a huge sweeping expanse of snow-covered glacier that flowed about at the base of the peak. The Sherpa, no longer in the lead, began dropping behind as Ed pressed eagerly forward.

The sun was up, and with it the wind began keening again, bitterly sharp, bringing with it a scent of coming snow. In the east, beyond the jagged peak just ahead, the immense escarpment of the Himalayas was lost in approaching cloud. Ed hurried as best he could; it would snow, and soon. He'd have to make better time.

But above the sky was blue, infinitely blue, and behind, the sun was well up, although the camp was still lost in night below. The peak thrust up ahead, near, with what appeared to be a natural pass skirting its flank. Ed made for it. As he circled an upthrust ridge of reddish rotten rock, he glanced ahead. The plateau spread out before him, gently sloping, a natural amphitheater full of deep smooth snow, with peaks surrounding it and the central peak thrusting a long, black shadow directly across the center. He paused, glancing back. The Sherpa had stopped well below him, his face a dark blur, looking up, gesticulating frantically, pointing to the clouds. Ed motioned, then moved around, leaning against the rock, peering ahead.

That great shadow against the snow was certainly similar to the one in the photo, only, of course, the shadow pointed west now, when later it would point northwest as the sun swung to the south. And when it did, most certainly it was the precise—. He sucked in a sharp, lung-piercing breath.

He stared, squinting against the rising wind that seemed to blow from earth's outermost reaches. Three figures stirred slightly and suddenly leaped into focus, almost perfectly camouflaged against the snow and wind-blasted rock. Three figures not more than a hundred feet below him. Two small, one larger.

He leaned forward, his heart thudding terribly at this twenty-thousand-foot height. A tremor of excitement shook him. My God, it was true. They existed. He was looking at what was undeniably a female and two smaller—what? Apes?

They were covered with downy hair, nearly white, resembling nothing so much as tight-fitting leotards. The female was exactly like any woman on earth except for the hair. No larger than most women, with arms slightly longer, more muscular. Thighs heavier, legs out of proportion to the trunk, shorter. Breasts full and firm.

Not apes.

Hardly breathing, Ed squinted, staring, motionless. Not apes. Not standing so erectly. Not with those broad, high brows. Not with the undeniable intelligence of the two young capering about their mother. Not—and seeing this, Ed trembled against the freezing rock—not with the sudden affectionate sweep of the female as she lifted the smaller and pressed it to her breast, smoothing back hair from its face with a motion common to every human mother on earth. A wonderfully tender gesture.

What were they? Less than human? Perhaps. He couldn't be certain, but he thought he heard a faint gurgle of laughter from the female, fondling the small one, and the sound stirred him strangely. Dr. Schenk had assured him that no animal was capable of genuine laughter; only man.

But they laughed, those three, and hearing it, watching the mother tickling the youngest one, watching its delighted squirming, Ed knew that in that marvelous little grouping below, perfectly lighted, perfectly staged, he was privileged to observe one of earth's most guarded secrets.

He should get started shooting his pictures; afterward, he should stun the group into unconsciousness with the gas gun and then send the Sherpa back down for Dr. Schenk and the others. Clouds were massing, immensities of blue black. Already the first few flakes of snow, huge, wet, drifted against his face.

But for a long moment more he remained motionless, oddly unwilling to do anything to destroy the harmony, the aching purity of the scene below, so vividly etched in brilliant light and shadow. The female, child slung casually on one hip, stood erect, hand shading her eyes, and Ed grinned. Artless, but perfectly posed. She was looking carefully about and above, scanning the great outcroppings of rock, obviously searching for something. Then she paused.

She was staring directly at him.

Ed froze, even though he knew he was perfectly concealed by the deep shadows of the high cliff behind him. She was still looking directly at him, and then, slowly, her hand came up.

She waved.

He shivered uncontrollably in the biting wind, trying to remain motionless. The two young ones suddenly began to jump up and down and show every evidence of joy. And suddenly Ed knew.

He turned slowly, very slowly, and with the sensation of a freezing knife plunging deeply into his chest he saw the male less than five yards away.

It was huge, by far twice the size of the female below. (And crazily Ed thought of Schenk's little lecture, given what seemed like eons ago, six weeks before, in the incredible tropical grove far below where rhododendrons grew in wild profusion and enormous butterflies flitted above: "In primitive man," Schenk had said, "as in the great apes today, the male was far larger than the female.")

The gas gun was hopelessly out of reach, securely strapped to his shoulder pack. Ed stared, knowing there was absolutely nothing he could do to protect himself before this creature, fully eight feet tall, with arms as big as Ed's own thighs and eyes (my God—*blue* eyes!) boring into his. There was a light of savage intelligence there—and something else.

The creature (man?) made no move against him, and Ed stared at it, breathing rapidly, shallowly and with difficulty, noting with his photographer's eyes the immense chest span, the easy rise and fall of his breathing, the large, square, white teeth, the somber cast of his face. There was long sandy fur on the shoulders, chest and back, shortening to off-white over the rest of the magnificent torso. Ears rather small and close to the head. Short, thick neck, rising up from the broad shoulders to the back of the head in a straight line. Toes long and definitely prehensile.

They looked silently at one another across the abyss of time and mystery. Man and—what? How long, Ed wondered, had it stood there observing him? Why hadn't it attacked? Had it been waiting for Ed to make a single threatening gesture such as pointing a gun or camera? Seeing the calm awareness in those long, slanting blue eyes, Ed sped a silent prayer of thanks upwards; most certainly if he had made a move for camera or gun, that move would have been his last.

They looked at one another through a curtain of falling snow, and suddenly there was a perfect, instantaneous understanding between them. Ed made an awkward, half-frozen little bow, moving backward. The great creature stood motionless, merely watching, and then Ed did a strange thing: he held out his hands, palm out, gave a wry grin and ducked quickly around the outcropping of rock and began a plunging, sliding return, down the way he'd come. In spite of the harsh, snow-laden wind, bitterly cold, he was perspiring.

Ed glanced back once. Nothing. Only the thickening veil of swift glowing snow blanking out the pinnacle, erasing every trace, every proof that anyone, anything, had stood there moments before. Only the snow, only the rocks, only the unending, wind-filled silence of the top of the world.

Nothing else.

The Sherpa was struggling up to him from below, terribly anxious to get started back; the storm was rising. Without a word they hooked up and began the groping, stumbling descent back to the last camp. They found the camp already broken, Sherpas already moving out. Schenk paused only long enough to give Ed a questioning look.

What could Ed say? Schenk was a scientist, demanding material proof. If not a corpse, at the very least a photograph. The only photographs Ed had were etched in his mind, not on film. And even if he could persuade Schenk to wait, when the storm cleared, the giant, forewarned, would be gone. Some farther peak, some remoter plateau would echo to his young ones' laughter.

Feeling not a bit bad about it, Ed gave Schenk a barely perceptible negative nod. Instantly Schenk shrugged, turned and went plunging down into the thickening snow, back into the world of littler men. Ed trailed behind.

On the arduous trek back through that first great storm, through the snowline, through the rain forest, hot and humid, Ed thought of the giant, back up there where the air was thin and pure.

Who, what were he and his race? Castaways on this planet, forever marooned, yearning for a distant, never-to-be-reached home?

Or did they date in unbroken descent from the Pleistocene, man's first beginning, when all the races of not-quite-man were giants, unable or unwilling to take the fork in the road that led to smaller, cleverer man; forced to retreat higher and higher, to more and more remote areas, until finally there was only one corner of earth left to them—the high Himalayas?

Or were he and his kind earth's last reserves; not-yet-men, waiting for the opening of still another chapter in earth's unending mystery story?

Whatever the giant was, his secret was safe with him, Ed thought. For who would believe it even if he chose to tell?

BEACH

XENOS BEACH

Graham Joyce

He went to the island to get as far away as he could from the rowdy parties of Ios and the commercialism of Mykonos. He'd had enough. The tourist season was smoked out and the recommended cure for heartbreak hadn't worked. The word was that this particular island had turned its back on tourists, that it neither needed nor wanted them, and that if you were not lying to yourself and you really did want to get away from it all, this was the place to go.

Sunlight lancing off the brilliant white paint of the hull had him squinting as he stepped off the inter-island ferry. Even in the dazzle the tiny port exhibited a post-industrial, neglected character. The place wasn't designed to take tourists and backpackers, and he had to step smartly around coils of rope and tarred capstans. Disinclined to practise his Greek on one of the grizzled old mariners languishing on the quayside, he dithered and scratched his head. Other passengers hurried away or were collected in rattletrap trucks. Only two minutes on the island and the long tooth of loneliness was beginning to bite.

Centuries of spice trading hung in the air of the old port. Dank warehouses of biscuit-coloured brick were crumbling into the water. Empty, cobwebby bars of fretwork shadows dotted the small waterfront, and the harbour slumbered under pearly, inspirational light.

He had a battered old *Giffords,* found on a Mykonos beach. As a tour guide its yellowing pages were hopelessly out of date, but he savoured the elegant Edwardian prose and its sniffy English reserve. About the island the book had very little to say, except to recommend that one should "quit the port at the earliest opportunity" and make for the west coast, where there were *mastic* villages and deserted, thrilling beaches. The island was the richest in Greece for *mastic*: the resin on the bushes crystallizes, harvested by the women, to be sold on for its aromatic properties. And on one of the beaches, the guidebook indicated, lay strewn the rubble of a marble temple to Aphrodite. The author claimed to have spent a sleepless night there under the stars.

At mid-day he climbed aboard a sweltering bus, sharing a seat with a crone in widow's black. Partially hooded by a dark cotton headscarf, her tooled-leather face could have been a thousand years old. On her lap rested a cardboard box, in which there was something live, black and feathery. The old woman dipped in a bag for seed, which she sucked in her toothless mouth, occasionally letting some of the seed fall into the box. At some point along the journey she offered him a seed, which he accepted and tried to nibble with good grace.

"*Pou pa?*" she asked energetically. "Where are you going?"

"Here." He pointed on his map.

She clucked at him. "Why? There are no bars. No tavernas. Nothing." She repeated the word for nothing with heavy emphasis. "Why go there?"

He wanted to explain a need for seclusion, but it was obvious she'd already decided he was a lunatic. The Greeks seemed to regard any solitary act, like hiking in the hills, as an expression of mental illness or depression; even in his own experience, a casual stroll would be quite likely to attract the desperate sympathy of an entire family who must then insist on keeping one company. Far better, he'd discovered, to lie about the purpose of your expedition and pretend to be going to see a man about a goat.

"Married?" she wanted to know. This familiarity was also normal for Greeks.

"Yes." He had no intention of going into detail about Alison.

"Children?"

"Yes," he lied, not wanting to evoke the universal sympathy accorded to the childless.

She spent the next few moments engaging every other passenger on the bus in his business. His Greek let him down as the pitch of her voice grew animated, even agitated. Everyone else was leaning forward and regarding him with rather too much interest. He still had the book open at the map. She tapped it vigorously and spat. Then she smacked her gums together conclusively. He was relieved when, along with most of the other passengers, his new acquaintance disembarked at one of the *mastic* villages.

When he came to get off the bus, the driver shook his head before driving off, leaving him standing in a cloud of diesel-exhaust on a parched, volcanic hillside.

Below the blue Aegean darted with sodium light. Hoisting backpack and tent, he descended the baked-earth path. It was some hike. Huge boulders ticked with heat. The hum of millions of insects among the stick-looking mountain vegetation was like the idling of a vast and invisible engine.

The climb down was almost two hours under a merciless sun. He thought about Alison. "There's only one solution to a woman who doesn't want you, and that's another woman." Peter had poured his advice like an after-dinner liqueur. "Go to Greece. Have some experiences. You'll get over her. Exhaust yourself on a romantic island with some beautiful French woman. Fall in love with a German goddess. Cry your eyes out over a Danish siren. Go to Greece. Visit the Gods."

He had swallowed Peter's prescription, hoping even that his classical studies in ancient Greek would help him get by. It didn't, but after making a fool of himself a few times he worked hard at the demotic. Four months had been spent island-hopping, camping, visiting the sights, the antiquities. Some days were lonely; some days were spent partying with people he didn't really want to be with. There *was* a dalliance with a beautiful Frenchwoman, and a night of shockingly rough passion with a Norwegian girl. Then towards the end of the season he woke, and not for the first time, with his face in the sand, his dry mouth tasting of aniseed, and decided the cure hadn't worked.

The worst night was when he found himself drunk and blubbering on a beach. A small dog, rib-thin and suffering from appalling mange, trotted across and licked his hand in pity. He stopped feeling sorry for himself, brought the dog a meal and phoned home to see how things stood.

Alison answered the phone and told him that she and Pete had got together. He laughed. For the first time in four months, he actually laughed. He laughed for so long he woke with his face in the sand for the second morning running. Then he decided to come to the island and do some thinking.

Approaching the bay he saw not the promised temple, but a tiny whitewashed Byzantine church with red terracotta roof. Higher up the beach of fine volcanic grey sand a fringe of trees marked off an area of deciduous scrub, contrasting emerald green with the barren ochre rock of the hillside above. The leaves of the scrub were peculiarly luminous and verdant, and he suspected that somewhere there he might find the sweetwater spring promised in his copy of *Giffords*.

The church was built in the center of the ruined temple. Fluted marble columns lay half-submerged in the sand, along with toppled capitals and broken plinths. Perhaps the Christian builders of the small church wanted to take advantage of the marble foundation; or maybe they sought to deactivate the power of the old gods. The tiny chapel itself had a dilapidated air as if it too were a relic of a broken culture. He tried the door. Unusually for an isolated Greek church, it was locked.

Deciding to pitch his tent under the shady protection of the trees, he moved further up the beach but was soon dismayed. It seemed he had company. Pitched between the trees at irregular intervals were six or seven other tents of differing shapes and sizes. All of the tents faced the sea, and in every case the original canvas or nylon colour had been bleached out by salt spray and harsh sunlight.

Passing by the tents, he tried to peek inside to see what kind of people were there, but the flaps were closed and there was no sound from within. Perhaps they were all in siesta, but there was no one swimming, and no other activity on the beach. After pitching his tent he went looking for the sweetwater spring, but couldn't locate it. He'd brought enough water for two or possibly three days if economical; but he had in mind staying a little longer. No one came out of the other tents, and no one returned to them either. Eventually the sunset turned the sea ember red, but after the sun had dipped under the water there was no moon and it quickly got cold. He cast about for wood to make a fire but he'd left it too late; so he climbed into his sleeping bag and read his *Giffords* by torchlight.

"A quite singular and beautiful cove," the *Giffords* reported, "but I do not care ever to return there."

Sometime in the night he was woken by a noise. He poked his head out of the tent. The sea, no more than twenty yards away, was calm, but there was still no moon. A light flickered, up at the other end of the beach, near the temple. The light hovered briefly, shifted, then it went out. He zipped up his tent and lay back, straining to listen for further sounds. Nothing. He opened his clasp knife and put it under his pillow.

In the morning he lay dozing in his sleeping bag, unable to surface. As the sun got up it became impossibly hot under the nylon and he wrenched himself awake. Tumbling out of the tent he walked like a somnambulist in an undeviating line to the sea. The water was chilly, effervescing on his skin. In the middle of snorting and splashing he suddenly remembered the other tents. There was still no sign of life. He'd hoped to be able to ask someone about water. Eventually he peeked inside the tent nearest to his own.

It was empty. So was the next. Examining them one by one he discovered the tents were all abandoned. No equipment had been left behind, nor any hint that their former occupants were about to return. Perhaps the local Greeks pitched them for convenient use at weekends or holiday times. It was October after all, and even though the days were still hot, the season was turning on the hinge of the Aegean autumn, and the nights could get very cold. No, he decided, he was alone, and with that realization a slight breeze picked up off the water. One of the tent-flaps fluttered in the airstream.

He went about naked. Eating only when hungry from the things he'd brought with him, he also went without cigarettes and alcohol for the first time in fifteen years. Much of the first day was spent searching for the fresh spring, without success. At the temple, on one of the marble blocks, he found the ugly carcass of a sea snake. Buzzing with flies, its razor-fine teeth were bared and its rotting scales gleamed magnificently. He found, under a stone, the key to the church.

Inside, a small icon hung on the wall above the altar, but the lamps were dust-covered and hadn't been lit for some time.

A bottle of oil and matches stood on a small table. He lit a lamp and a breath of light seemed to sigh around the tiny chamber. The flame winked on the silver icon. The face enclosed in the silver frame, one of the patriarchs of Greek orthodoxy, seemed stirred to anger rather than to one of the tender emotions. He got out, but left the lamp burning.

Soon it was dusk and this time he had his fire assembled ready for the dark. He was just finishing up a meal of olives, bread and cheese when he saw a dark flag-like figure by the water's edge. Again the dying sun had turned the water the colour of live coals. The figure approached in silhouette, his back to the sun, seemingly clothed in flapping black rags. A thrill of alarm passed through him with unnecessary force.

It was a Greek Orthodox priest. For some reason he didn't feel comforted. His skin flushed. The priest carried his stovepipe hat in his hand, his pace diminishing as he came closer. Finally he stood off by a good few yards.

"*Yia sas!*" he said to the priest, forcing a smile, "*Yia!*"

"*Yia sas*," the priest echoed quietly, eyeing him suspiciously, peering round him at the tent. A single bead of sweat ran darkly between the priest's eyebrows.

Even though as a traveler he was the *xenos,* the stranger, he tried to offer the priest some of the food he'd been eating. This desperate parody of Greek courtesy irritated the priest, who declined with a gesture. "What are you doing?" he asked.

"Camping." He wanted to add something rude. He'd taken a huge and irrational dislike to the priest.

"It's not a good place for that."

"Why?"

The question was ignored. "What do you do here?"

"I swim. I fish." It was true; he'd brought a hand-line along and hoped to catch something.

"Dangerous to swim here. Very dangerous. There are currents out there that can take you out to sea. Very dangerous."

Not having noticed any currents while swimming in the bay earlier, he raised his eyebrows at the priest. "Can you show me where there is water?"

"Water?"

"Yes! Water! For drinking! My book says there's fresh water somewhere." The priest, startled by this sudden animation, was torn by how to respond and merely mopped his sweating brow. "For goodness sake, it's only water!"

The priest unaccountably turned his back and began to retrace his steps. He leapt to his feet and followed. "How long are you staying here?" the priest barked over his shoulder.

"Not long."

When they reached the temple, the priest led him behind the marble blocks and grudgingly pointed to a slab. "There. But it's brackish."

Watched by the priest he removed the slab to uncover a shallow well. With a cupped hand he drew out a few drops of water. It tasted fresh and cool and clear. The priest's nostrils began to twitch as if he was sniffing the air. "Have you been burning *mastic*?" he demanded angrily, mopping his brow with a handkerchief.

"Why would I do that?"

"Are you certain?"

"Of course I'm certain!"

He'd had enough of this priest who, scowling, went inside the church and closed the door. He retreated up the beach. Some time later when he returned to the church, it was locked and the priest had gone.

He lit a fire and pretty soon had a decent blaze going, though the piles of thin scrub flared too quickly. Crackling fiercely, it sent white sparks arcing across the fire before burning smokily. Very soon he realized what the priest had been talking about. The incense-rich smell of burning *mastic* was everywhere.

He'd unwittingly piled dead *mastic* bushes on his fire. The entire beach already smelled like a gargantuan temple. Flames writhed in the dark, flinging indigo shadows across the sand, and with the waves crowding nearer behind his back the fire assumed a sacramental quality. He sat with a blanket around his shoulders, hypnotized by the flames, drugged by perfumed smoke. He felt his forehead: his temperature was high.

When he awoke sweating in his tent the next morning he had no recollection of having gone to bed. Outside, his fire had burned out, and he stumbled across the sand and into the cold water, where he was shocked properly awake. While brushing his teeth in seawater he spotted activity at the other end of the beach.

Three or four figures, perhaps a family, were busy close to the temple. Conscious of his own nakedness, he splashed through the water and jogged back to his tent, where he pulled on some shorts. He sat in his tent, wondering what to do.

Of course, he didn't have to *do* anything. They were campers, just like him. Perhaps they would cook *souvlaki* on a barbecue, stay for an hour or two and go home. What difference could it make? Concerned to announce his presence, he hit on the solution of going to draw some water from the spring.

He carried his water bottle the length of the beach. Four figures were busy with something on the ground. Rather than occupying one of the available tents, they had rigged up a large but crude shelter, immediately adjacent to the temple. Advertising his presence by a noisy approach, he actually got quite close before one of them looked up. Then all four of them stopped what they were doing and gaped back at him, open-mouthed.

He had the uncanny sensation that he was himself a ghost.

The older of the two men rose very slowly and stared, his hands hanging loose at his sides.

"*Yia sas.*"

"*Yia sas,*" they replied, in precise and hasty concert.

"Where did you come from?" the older man said quickly, still in a state of astonishment. The accent was difficult, but just comprehensible. They were gypsies in all probability. When the tent at the far end of the beach was pointed out the man stepped forward, his eyes followed the line of the pointing finger. His manly perspiration was strong and blended with an overpowering scent of *mastic*. Then one of the women spoke rapidly. Only the word *philoxenia* stood out, like a bright pearl among flat stones, before the man gestured to a sharing of the meal they were preparing. They had been slicing some kind of offal on a marble slab. It looked less than appetizing.

The older man went into the rough tent and came out proffering a pottery tumbler filled to the brim with blood-red wine. It was slightly salty, acidic and rather thick, but it was to be drunk. Reciprocation of Greek hospitality demanded so. It was after all entirely possible that they were entertaining one of the Gods unawares, and he should behave as if he believed that to be the case. He tipped back the wine and they immediately seemed to relax; except for the younger man, who seemed unable to do anything but stare.

It was difficult not to stare back. The family was distinctive from most Greeks. These were darker skinned, and yet with copper hair, totally unlike the blueblack of most island Greeks. But they were not of the Asiatic descent seen in the islands close to Turkey. Gypsies, surely. He had to make a conscious effort to avoid gazing at the younger of the two women. His eyes returned to her time and again as they ate slices of cooked heart and liver, during which the older couple plied him with questions about his former life.

"From England? England, you say?" It was as if he'd stipulated that he had recently arrived from the lost city of Atlantis. Meanwhile the younger man maintained a hostile silence.

He noticed that the locked door of the chapel had been kicked down. He could see the priest's hat and cloak and shoes strewn around the floor. It was while he took in this disturbing detail that he felt a hand lightly brush his shoulder. "Will you swim with me?" the younger woman asked, smiling.

She ran the same hand through her hair and the sun flaked fire around her. He felt a jab to the viscera. Her fingers playing with her hair were uncommonly long. Her white teeth flashed; the heavy lashes of her oval eyes blinked lazily.

"Swim! Swim!" said the father, waving towards the water.

"Will you swim with us?" he asked the younger man, trying to make some sort of point, but the fellow shook his head contemptuously, picked up a handline and jogged to the waters' edge.

The young woman set off up the beach. "It's better this way," she murmured. None of her group seemed inclined to follow, and the two of them clambered over some rocks, going out of view of the others. There she slipped of her rough costume and waded in, her shins swishing through the water.

He blinked at the naked girl. She had a large birthmark on her bottom. As he slipped off his own trunks and followed her she waited, her eyes unashamedly assessing his body. Unconsciously, or perhaps not, she moistened her lips with her tongue. When he drew abreast of her she turned in a smooth motion and made an elegant crawl stroke through the water. Following, he found it difficult to keep up, feeling the tug of a strong undertow. The priest hadn't been lying about the swift currents. Afraid, he swam back alone.

He sat on the shoreline panting hard, trying to spot her. Alarmed over her safety he considered calling the others, but at last he descried a tiny dot returning from far out. Eventually she fell down beside him, uncomfortably close. Hardly out of breath she said, "But you didn't come all the way!" A teasing note in her voice.

"Not me."

She squeezed water from her hair and it trickled down the ridge of her spine, where he wanted to brush his fingers. With her toes dipped in the water she wriggled her bottom deeper into the grey sand. A strong whiff of *mastic* incense came off the girl. Again his skin flushed, as it had in the presence of the priest, but differently this time. It was as if some warning chill came off her, some marine odour alerting him to a danger he had no capacity to understand. She locked eyes with him, and her breathing became shallower. He wanted to lean across and take the dark, erect berry of her nipple in his mouth. Too afraid, he asked her name.

"Alethea." She stepped back into her beach garb. An important moment had slipped.

But he was glad he hadn't chanced his arm, because seconds later the young man appeared. He paced by, scowling, suspicious. A fishing line trailed from his wrist, and swinging from the hook was a vicious looking sea-snake, jaw open, fangs bared, exactly like the specimen rotting by the temple. A wave of hostility emanated from the young man as he passed, and it occurred to him that he'd made a mistake.

The situation was unclear. "Is that your brother?" he asked Alethea.

"Of course."

So why, he wanted to ask, is he behaving like a jealous lover? But after all, he was the *xenos* here, the one who didn't know the rules. Perhaps her nudity was innocent. Perhaps only her brother of all of them guessed the sensational effect she was having on an outsider.

For the next two or three days he ate, drank and swam with the family. They made fires in the evening and in the incense clouds they talked little. He went on long walks with Alethea. Together they explored nearby beaches, rock-pools and sea-caves, all of the time their hands almost touching and he never once thought of England or of Alison.

One afternoon, as they waded between rocks carpeted with slippery, luminous green weed, both naked having been swimming, Alethea missed her footing and grabbed his arm. It was the first time they had touched. Again he felt a visceral punch and a white-hot flare in his brain before he pressed his mouth roughly to hers, tasting salt-spray on her lips, scenting that strange mixture of marine odour and incense. Her hand cupped around his genitals. At that moment Alethea's brother chose to reveal himself.

Leaping from behind a rock he ran at them, puce in the face, screaming incomprehensible insults. But he failed to follow through, and quickly stalked away.

"It was only a kiss!"

Alethea looked stung and betrayed.

He knew he was wrong. "No. It wasn't only a kiss," he said. "I want to be with you."

"You can't," she said simply. "Let's go back."

They walked hand in hand along the sand, but she let go as they approached her family. Her brother was still red-faced and angry. Her mother too looked furious, but her father, scratching the back of his leathery neck, looked sad. An impenetrable conversation began which he couldn't follow, though several times he heard them refer to him in the usual way.

At last he said, "I want to be with your daughter. I'm prepared to do anything it takes."

"It's not that simple," her father said.

"What could be more simple?"

"You don't understand. You are a stranger. Even if you

were one of the local Greeks from this island, it would still be impossible."

"Is it because you are gypsies?"

"Gypsies? Ha!"

"And anyway," the boy spat, "you are not worthy!"

A furious quarrel broke out between the family, bitter and vindictive. Alethea broke away and ran up the beach. He went to go after her, but her father held him by the arm. "Leave her. It's no good. It's no good *for you*."

He shrugged off the old man and took off after Alethea. She'd gone beyond the rocks on to the next bay. "What do they mean?" he asked when he caught up with her. "Why do they say these things?"

She shook her head. They sat on the sand holding each other, she staring out to sea at some invisible point on the horizon. At last she said, "I sometimes think they don't want me to have anyone."

"Has this happened before?"

She nodded sadly, and he felt profoundly disappointed to be a second-comer. "They won't allow us to put this beach behind us."

He nodded, trying to accommodate the Greek figure of speech.

"No, you don't understand at all. It isn't just a way of speaking. It means lovers must go on, to another beach." She pointed out to sea, to a rock barely discernible in the distance. "To that beach. But I don't think you can make it."

It dawned on him that she was being quite literal. Some kind of gypsy ritual perhaps, a rite-of-passage for a courting couple.

"Swim? You mean swim to that rock? What are you saying?"

"We could get away. I would be at your side, swimming with you."

She was proposing an elopement! He slumped to the sand and sat with his head in his hands. "But that's out of the question!"

"Why?"

He had to think about it, but his head was on fire. She was actually inviting him to elope, and he couldn't think of a single reason why they shouldn't. The gravity of the moment pounded the beach like a wave. She was still searching his eyes for an answer. It shocked him that he was being offered a truly spontaneous moment of decision, in which he could make something astonishing happen or lose her forever. He'd been granted a miraculous opportunity to redeem his life with a single passionate act.

And yet what she proposed was madness. It was heady and dangerous. He looked at the rock in the distance, trying to calculate the swim. Last time he'd tried something like that he'd turned back exhausted at far less than half the distance. He feared the currents. But that phrase haunted, the one about "putting the beach behind him." He thought of the uselessness and the sadness of his life back in England. He had nothing to return to there. He gave no thought to what happened once the rock was reached. He assumed at that point that the statement had been made, that they would cross a symbolic or ritual line beyond which no challenge could be made to them. Then they would swim back.

Drunk on the romance of the situation, and on the

reckless inspiration of her youth, he took one last look round. In the few days he'd been camping on the beach the dye had been almost bleached from his tent. It only convinced him to leave it all with the row of other tattered tents abandoned under the fringe of trees.

"You don't have to do this," Alethea said.

He said nothing. She stripped off her costume and waded out into the water. Not until she was waist deep did she turn and beckon him to follow.

The water was buoyant and he felt strong. They swam for a long time. He even felt the sun shifting in the sky. Once out of a sense of anxiety, he tried to look back to the shore, but Alethea rebuked him. After swimming for almost two hours, the distant rock seemed no nearer.

He began to feel cold. Then he felt the undertow strike, and despite his efforts, began to sense he was failing to make progress. The distance between him and Alethea increased.

For the first time since they'd set out he took a lungful of water. Coughing and thrashing about, he had to rescue himself from a moment of panic. The distance between them widened, though he could hear her exhorting him to stay close. In a thrill of horror he wondered if she might abandon him; because he also sensed that if she didn't make the pace then they would both fail. The current was sweeping him to the side. He couldn't make progress and found it impossible to swim in her wake.

His muscles ached. While trying to lie on his back to snatch a moment's rest the current dragged and flipped him back on his stomach. He took another lungful of water. When he looked back he could barely discern the shore.

And when he turned, he heard the cry of a gull and Alethea was gone.

Calling her name and struggling against the current he lost all sense of direction. He swam desperately in the bearing he thought she had gone, his muscles turning to a fiery, unresolved slush and his feet cramping. The cold was penetrating and primal.

He despaired. Shouting her name again, in his panic and confusion he heard himself calling not for her, but for Alison. It was all too much; not just the swim, but everything that had driven him to this island, and to this pass. In his overwhelming tiredness he felt a tremendous desire to simply close his eyes. The possibility of surrender seemed at last sweet and comforting. He dropped his arms into the water, the better to accept the chilly sleep.

But anger sparked him awake again. Turning, he tried to swim. Still the current dragged. He took a lungful of air, and dived down, trying to swim under the surface tow, finding he could make better progress that way. He surfaced, breathed deep and dived again. He did this several times, until he had escaped the spiralling current. Catching sight of the headland, he made agonizing progress towards it.

Then the land was before him. It was not the distant rock: he'd returned to his starting point. The sun was setting, the sea was burning ember-red. Crawling out of the water on hands and knees, he collapsed, shuddering, weeping, clawing and biting at the sand with relief. The gritty particles of sand under his fingernails were like grains of light, jewels of deliverance, shredded tokens of the life he had almost thrown away in this desperately stupid act.

When he woke it was dark. He got to his feet and staggered up the beach. He was alone. Desperate for water he cast around in the dark trying but failing to locate the spring. Returning to his tent he found a drop of water in a plastic bottle. Shivering uncontrollably he unrolled his sleeping bag and climbed inside.

When morning came around, his muscles were on fire. He lay sweating under the nylon, thinking about what he'd done. His head pounded. He got out of the tent and went to find water. There was neither spring nor the stone slab which had covered it. It was absurd: both himself and Alethea's family had been sustained by the spring over several days.

Alethea's family had made a tidy departure. There was no trace of them, not even an impression in the sand of where they'd been sheltered. Neither was there any sign of their campfire. The charred remains and blackened stones of his own fire were there, sure enough, further along the beach, but where was the evidence of the fire around which he'd spent those few happy evenings? The sun pulsed directly overhead. Sand gusted along the beach.

He decamped hurriedly. The bus which had delivered him there was due to pass again that afternoon. At the temple he saw what was perhaps the only evidence of the gypsy family's presence. A second decomposing sea snake lay on a broken plinth, next to the first one he'd seen, almost like an offering.

For the last time he glanced back at the row of tattered tents, and again he wondered to whom they belonged. Hoisting his pack he made the climb up the hillside. At the roadside he sat on his pack until the bus came, and flagged it to stop.

It was the same driver. He looked somewhat surprised, and when asked for water he produced a tin of Sprite from a cool-box. "Take it. Where have you been all these days?"

"Down on the beach."

"Alone?"

He started to explain that there had been other people, and that a priest had shown him where to find water, and that—

"Priest? There is no priest on this side of the island."

The driver stared blankly then crunched through his gears as the bus moved up the hill. After that he would only look at his passenger through the rear-view mirror.

"I wouldn't go to that beach," he said.

"Why not?"

He merely shook his head. As they travelled back across the island, stopping at the *mastic* villages with their singular, geometrically patterned houses, the stranger thought of the last few days, and of Alethea. He wondered where she was. He thought also of the row of tattered tents under the trees, and wondered if he had narrowly escaped something deeply danger-ous; or if he had forfeited some experience transcendent and beautiful.

FOREST

DEATH TO THE EASTER BUNNY

Alan Ryan

When Paul and I and the girls met the old man in the woods that day, we never thought we'd end up living here in the mountains. Of course, we never thought we'd have to kill the Easter Bunny either.

The four of us—that's Paul and Susanne, and Barbara and me—had been looking for some place we could go on weekends that wouldn't cost too much or be too far from New York. When we found Deacons Kill, about four hours north in the Catskills, we knew right away it was the kind of place we wanted. It's mostly dairy farms and wooded hills and plain, decent people. The town is nice too; it's small and everybody's pretty friendly and there's a great old hotel, called the Centennial Hotel, right on the village square. As soon as we discovered the Kill—that's what everybody calls the town—last winter, we started coming up all the time.

So there we were one day, the four of us walking along some backwoods road, just strolling because it was pretty cold and we didn't want to get too far away from where we'd left the car, and Susanne was complaining that she wasn't dressed warmly enough and Barbara was saying her new boots hurt her feet. Then Paul saw a small trail leading into the woods among the pine trees and he wanted to follow it a little way.

There was some discussion back and forth and finally we agreed to go a short distance, maybe five minutes' worth of walking, before turning back. Actually, I would have preferred to be back in our room at the Centennial Hotel with Barbara, just the two of us, but if I hadn't given in to Paul that time, we might never have met the old man and the Easter Bunny would still be running around and none of this would be happening.

We had gone only a little distance in among the pines when suddenly a voice called out and it was clearly yelling at us, no mistake about it.

"That's enough! Hold it right there!"

It wasn't so much the suddenness of it, or even the *sound* of it, that stopped us right in our tracks. It was really just the voice of an old man, rough and a little gravelly, but still just the voice of an old man. The thing that got to all of us as soon as we heard it, though, was the *tone*. It sounded like a lot of things all at once: angry, exasperated, determined, threatening. And frightened. It sounded frightened. The four of us stood rock still right where we were.

"What are you doing here? You don't belong here!"

I turned around to see where the voice was coming from and there was the old man. I'm not old enough to remember Gabby Hayes but I've seen pictures of him and this old man looked a little like that. Or maybe a little like the way we think of Rip Van Winkle. He had a beard that was gray and stringy, and his eyes were bright and had wrinkles all around them and his clothes were the color of the woods, gray and brown and no color in particular, and he was pointing a double-barreled rifle at the four of us.

"Holy shit!" Paul said behind me.

"What are you doing here?" the old man said again, and he panned the rifle back and forth like a movie camera. I could see his finger in the trigger.

"Hold on!" I said. "We're not doing anything. We were just taking a walk."

The old man stared at me pretty skeptically for a few seconds. I was thinking fast, or trying to, and wishing Paul would say something clever. Nobody had ever pointed a gun at me before. Mostly I was thinking that if the old guy really fired it, I'd be the first to get it, which I guess is a pretty selfish thought. But before I could think of what to say, the old man lowered the rifle and pointed it at the ground. That was when my knees started feeling weak and my heart started pounding. Behind me, I heard Barbara say, "Oh, my God," and I discovered that I had put one hand behind me to sort of protect her. She grabbed it and held it tight.

"What are you doing here?" the old man asked again, but he sounded less angry this time than he had before. I could almost have thought he sounded a little relieved.

I told him again that we had only been taking a walk, yes, in winter, we didn't mind the cold, we hoped we weren't trespassing, no, we weren't carrying guns, yes, we were planning on going right back out to the road, and so on and so on, with Paul helping out now with the answers, and finally the old man began to look like nothing more than just an old man who happened to be carrying a rifle.

It was Paul who asked the question, and, when he did, I could have kicked him for it.

"What are *you* doing here?" he said to the old man. "Do you own these woods?"

The old man looked at Paul very hard, then he looked at me, then at Barbara and Susanne, and then back at Paul again. You could almost see him making up his mind whether we were challenging him or not, or just asking, the way anybody might. I kept my eye on the rifle barrel but it stayed pointed at the ground.

The old man studied the four of us a little longer, then he said, "I own these woods as much as anybody does. Maybe more." There was a sort of stony grimness in the way he said it.

There was a kind of impasse at that point, him studying us and us studying him right back again. Then I could see his posture lose some of its tenseness and for the first time I knew we were really out of trouble.

I think it was Barbara who said something next, asked him a question maybe, and after that it was a fairly normal conversation, considering the circumstances. It wasn't exactly a prize-winning conversation or anything like that, like you might have in a good bar late at night, but we were all chatting more or less easily with him after a minute or so.

That first meeting seems even stranger now. I really don't know what we could have been talking about, and the others don't remember either (I guess we were still nervous from the way he'd scared us), except I know he said something about "intruders" a couple of times, meaning intruders into his woods. I do remember thinking that he sounded as if he might even get to be friendly after a while, even though we didn't learn anything about him at all. For all we found out that time, he might have lived in the trees. As it turned out, that wouldn't have been a bad guess.

When the conversation, if you can call it that, was starting to wear down, the old man said, and I do remember this part very clearly, "You can stop by again when you're this way." Then he added, more quietly, "I'll be here."

That's how it started.

Naturally we talked about the old man a lot that weekend and other times afterward. And of course we talked about it the next time the four of us went up there, which was a couple of weeks later.

We had only been in the hotel a little while on Friday evening. Barbara and I were still unpacking and putting clothes away and Barbara was upset because a blouse she wanted to wear to dinner on Saturday had gotten crushed in the suitcase. And we were fooling around a little too while we unpacked. There was a knock at the door and I opened it and Susanne and Paul came in.

Paul plopped himself down on one of the chairs by the window and Susanne sat on his knee and Paul said, "Let's go see that weird old guy in the woods."

"You have got to be kidding," I said right away, but the truth is, I'd been thinking about doing that myself but not saying anything because I thought the others would think I was crazy.

Paul was serious. "I am not kidding," he said. "I want to go see him. I think"—and here Paul got a really solemn and serious look on his face and the same kind of sound in his voice— "that it was nothing less than fate that brought us to him. Fate, I tell you. Kismet. We are *intended* to know the old coot and have all sorts of wonderful adventures with him." Paul teaches English, which explains a lot.

Well, we talked about it for a while and Barbara and Susanne and I all said we didn't want any part of it and the weather was too cold to go traipsing around in the woods anyway, but it turned out that none of us really meant it, so in the end we decided we'd go back and find that trail and see if the old man would actually be there again.

And so on Saturday we drove out to that same road and found the trail and started along it. We were all pretty nervous the farther we went, and we had to go a long way this time before anything happened—so far, in fact, that we were all starting to think that maybe we had imagined the old man in the first place or maybe he had only been a local farmer or a drifter who was having some fun at our expense. But of course just at the point when we were starting to talk about turning back toward the road, because it really was very cold that day, the old man stepped out from behind a tree—at least, that's what we thought when we talked about it later—and stood there on the path in front of us.

He didn't say anything right away this time, just looked at us. He still had the rifle but it was pointing at the ground.

I don't think any of us had actually believed that we'd see him again. But there he was, looking just the same as before.

The old man sort of nodded his head a little bit, which I took to be a greeting. Paul had been leading the way and was closest, so he was the first to speak.

"Hello," he said. "Bet you thought you'd never see us again." Which wasn't a very brilliant thing to say, but it suddenly made me realize for the first time that we had never learned the old man's name.

"Bet you thought you'd never see *me* again," the old man said. He wasn't smiling.

We shuffled around a little at that, because of course it was true. The next thing I remember is that we were talking with the old fellow again, the way we had the other time, easy and natural—talking about the woods, I guess, because I can't think what else it might have been. It's always happened that way, then and since, and it always seems so weird later on: standing there in the woods, first in winter and later in spring and summer and so on, talking with him for a while but not remembering a word of what was said.

But I do remember clearly him saying, "Come home with me."

I know we followed him off the trail and deep into the woods and I know that we did some climbing up the hillsides (and I know that he had to lead us out to the path afterward), but I have no clear picture in my mind of how we got to his home, that first time or any of the other times.

When I think about it now, I have to admit that I don't understand either why we actually went with him in the first place. But we did. He led the way and we followed.

The old man lives way up high on a hill, in the very darkest and thickest part of the woods, the sort of place where you can almost imagine the Big Bad Wolf jumping out and attacking Little Red Riding Hood. The sort of place you dream about when you're a child . . . at least that's the best recollection of it I ever have. It's never really clear afterward, no more than it was that first time. It was as if a cloud or a mist surrounded the spot, hiding its details from us, while allowing us to glimpse just enough to make us think it was not-so-strange and not-so-scary. It might have been a shed or a cabin or a huge old mansion in the woods. It might have been a cave or a wooden structure in the treetops. It might have been none of those things. We didn't know then and we don't know now. But the old man somehow always made it all right.

Inside it was the same: vague, yet clear, real and unreal, not warm and not cold, odd and not-so-strange. That first time, the old man invited us to sit—there were things to sit on but I don't know what they were—and he gave us something to drink—something neither hot nor cold—but I don't know what it was.

And he talked. He talked about the hills and about the

woods and rivers and streams and the trees and the rocks and the dirt, talked about the wildness of nature and its order, its beauty, its bestiality, about the air and the weather and about storms and rains and snows and winds.

We listened—that first time, as I remember, and every time since then—in thrall.

And he talked about the city, about how the city was different from the country and about how we had to learn the ways of the hills, and somehow we knew that he was right.

And after a while he led us out of the woods and we were back on the trail and then at the road and then at the car, and the four of us were looking at each other kind of funny, a little embarrassed, and none of us wanted to be the first to say that it had really happened or that it hadn't, but of course we knew it had.

"Holy shit!" Paul said softly when we were safely in the car.

Nobody said anything else just then, but we talked plenty when we got back to the Centennial. But that doesn't mean we knew what to make of it all, especially when the four of us realized that we had no clear idea of why we had gone with the old man or of how he had led us through the woods. Or of what his house—if it was a house—had looked like. Or of what we had talked about with him. None of it was clear, none of it made any logical kind of sense.

The one thing we knew for certain was that, after the first few seconds with the old man, we hadn't been afraid.

"He's some kind of sorcerer," Paul said, but he wouldn't look any of us in the eye as he said it.

"There's no such thing," Barbara said. "Don't be ridiculous." Barbara teaches physics and has no patience with stuff like that. She's a good sport, which is one of the things I like most about her, but she can be pretty sharp about things she considers dumb.

"Listen," Paul said, and he put on his most casual expression and turned to face Barbara because he knew she was the biggest skeptic among the four of us. "I'm not saying I believe what I just said, but I'm not saying I don't either."

"That's a nice clear statement," Barbara said. I could see she was getting edgy.

"Come on, listen," Paul said. "Let's just examine this, okay? We meet a weird old guy in the woods. First he scares the hell out of us, sneaking up the way he did. Then he turns out to be all right. We talk with him for a while and——"

"——and after that we don't remember what happened," Barbara said quickly.

"I'm talking about the first time," Paul said.

"I'm talking about *both* times," Barbara answered.

Paul looked uncomfortable. "Well, okay, but that's part of it. I mean, the fact that we don't remember clearly what happened sort of suggests . . ." Paul hesitated, then grinned, then shrugged. "Maybe he put a spell on us."

"Oh God," Barbara said. "I don't believe this."

"It fits."

Barbara looked away from him.

"It fits," Paul said again.

"All this fresh country air is beginning to rot your brain," Barbara said, by which I knew she was beginning to give in.

"What do you think, Greg?" Susanne asked me. "You've been keeping pretty quiet."

I'd been keeping quiet because I'd been having the same sort of crazy ideas Paul was having, and I figured I'd let him be the one to put it into words. "I say it's as good an explanation as any. We'll just have to be sharp next time, maybe take notes or pictures or something, and then see what's going on."

The others nodded, and then suddenly we were all staring at each other and Barbara was squeezing my hand very tight. We hadn't talked about going back, hadn't said a word about it, but I'd just said "next time," and we all knew that we would.

That was in February and it was the beginning of March, about three weeks later, before we went back to Deacons Kill and saw the old man again.

Barbara had been playing basketball with the girls in her homeroom and had sprained her ankle so that she had to have it taped up for a couple of weeks. I went to the doctor with her when the bandages were taken off. The doctor said her ankle was fine now, and as soon as we were outside in the car, Barbara said, "Well, I'm ready," and I knew what she meant. I called Paul as soon as I got home and he said he'd tell Susanne—he didn't have far to go because I could hear her saying something in the background—and they'd be ready to roll on Friday. The only other thing we talked about was whether we'd take his car or mine.

Apart from that, we didn't say a single word about the old man the whole time we were back in the city.

It all happened just the same, except for one thing. This time, afterward, we remembered what the old man had talked to us about. At least, I did. I remembered it very clearly. The others didn't say so and I never said a word, not even to Barbara, but I could tell that they remembered too. We were all sort of avoiding each other's eyes and I could just tell.

He talked about intruders again, the way he had the first time we'd met him. He talked about how the world was filled with strange creatures, strange *beings,* living things that are alive in a way that's different from everything else in the world, and that therefore don't belong at all in the real world, don't fit into the human world, and how we have to get rid of them, how they pervert our minds and distort our view of reality. It made a lot of sense, the way he explained it. I can still hear his voice that time, low and soft but with a kind of hard tenseness in it. He knew what he was talking about. He said his life was devoted to ridding the world of these intruders. And he said that they were too much, too strong, for one old man alone and that he needed help to do it and that he had chosen us.

He didn't mention the Easter Bunny that time.

When he said he needed to see us again in a week, we all said together that we'd be there.

* * *

This was the time he first mentioned the Easter Bunny.

The four of us were sitting in the old man's . . . let's call it house, because by now we were able to see it more clearly than we had before. We were still vague about the route up the hill from the trail and the exact location of the house and what it looked like outside. But the inside was now clear enough for us to see it. The walls were very rough—maybe stone or some strange kind of logs—and there were no windows, but there were rugs or animal skins of some sort on the floor and plenty of places to sit, chairs and benches, although most often we just sat in a circle in the middle of a very big room, all five of us, while the old man talked.

Gradually, as we were there more and more often, we began asking questions, rather than just listening to him talk. He told us one time that he was very happy at having selected us and that he was glad we were getting into the spirit of it, glad that we were showing real progress and that we were beginning to understand the danger that threatened the world. That was what he called it: the danger that threatened the world.

He was very convincing when he spoke. I know he didn't pull any tricks on us, like hypnotism or something. I'm sure he did nothing of the sort. All I know is that he convinced us—and it seemed very clear, right from the start—that he had been waiting for us to come along and that . . . that we had been looking for him.

It's all very strange. After all, the four of us are just pretty ordinary people, like anybody else. We're not weird or anything, we don't belong to any crazy religious sects, we don't give a hoot about astrology or tarot cards or stuff like that, nothing crazy or freaky at all. We're all pretty bright, I guess, and pretty well educated, but that's certainly in our favor. At least, it makes it less likely that the old man could be playing any tricks on us, either then or now.

The simple fact was that everything he said made sense. It all made sense. And by the time he finished telling us about the Easter Bunny, we knew what he meant when he spoke about danger, danger that threatened the world.

Barbara was the one who said it first to the old man. "A lot of people," she said, keeping her voice very steady, "say the Easter Bunny is just imaginary."

The old man smiled patiently at her and then at the rest of us. "You see," he said softly. "You see what I mean. That's just the sort of thing I'm talking about. That monster comes out of hiding, tramps as free as you please all over the world, and yet he has people convinced that he doesn't even exist. It's amazing what these creatures can do to the human mind! Absolutely amazing! And terrifying." He leaned forward into the circle, his eyes sweeping slowly over the four of us as he spoke. "You do see, don't you? I know you do. Just think about it. If you asked any-body, anybody at all, they could tell you, I'm sure, what the Easter Bunny looks like, more or less. And of course, they all think he's very . . . well, they'd use words like *cute* and *cuddly* and *sweet*. Imagine! And yet, if you asked them whether or not he exists, they'd all say that he doesn't, that he's just a creature of myth or something. But children, small children, know per-fectly well that he exists and they'll tell you so with no hesita-tion. Children are much closer to that sort of knowledge, they have an instinctive awareness of strange, primitive things like that. And if you stop to think about it, you know that there isn't a child in the world that would stand still and smile if he saw the Easter Bunny actually come around a corner and walk toward him. You know that child would run for its life. Well, children know these things and understand them. Oh yes, children know. It's only later on, as they grow older, that their minds become clouded, that they forget the most important things, the special kinds of instinctive knowledge they had when they were so young, before the world took hold of their minds. But they know. Children know. And they know enough to be afraid."

We were breathless at his speech, at the intensity of it, the fear in his voice, the determination to make us understand, to rip away the veil of adulthood that might cloud our eyes, to convince us of the need for action. It was a special moment and we were all frozen in silence when he finished speaking.

"How do you know?" Barbara said. Always the skeptic, from force of habit, but I could tell by the look on her face that she believed.

"I am different," the old man answered gently. "I am special. I can see clearer than others. And I can help you see."

We were nodding, convinced already. Barbara nodded too.

"When the time comes," the old man said, his voice barely a whisper because he was clearly exhausted from tension, "when the time comes, I will show you and you will know it for yourselves."

When he led us from the house to the trail later that day, the misty woods seemed alive with flitting spirits and shifting shadows.

* * *

We went to the woods every weekend after that.

Between trips, we never talked about it among ourselves. Talk like that was only for the forest, for the old man's house in the woods, and for the safety of his home and his presence.

The weather was still bad sometimes in March, but then at the beginning of April it began to get a little warmer, and here and there a little fresh green color began to appear at the edges of the roads in Deacons Kill. The woods themselves were still very dark and very bare, except for the firs, and damp because of the rain in April. When the old man led us up from the trail each weekend, we didn't even try to see the way. The woods were too frightening, too filled with malevolent spirits and creatures only half alive.

"The time is coming," the old man reminded us each week.

Easter Sunday would be at the end of April and we grew more and more tense as it approached.

Two weeks before it, the old man put us to work. He started by taking us outside his house for the first time. He surveyed the woods carefully—they were so thick, so strangely dense right there around the house, that it was impossible to see more than a few feet away. He chose several young trees and we cut them down and stripped them, all under his careful supervision, and brought the straight trunks inside. He instructed us in how to whittle the end down to a very sharp, very hard point, and how to trim the shaft to make a firm handhold. We prepared four of them for each of us, twenty in all. We worked at it for two weekends and then we were ready for Easter.

* * *

Since school was closed for the holiday, we got an early start on Good Friday. Our four-hour car trips up to Deacons Kill had grown very quiet in recent weeks, but this one was absolutely silent. The only sound we heard was the tires against the highway. We all knew what lay ahead and we were all, I'm sure, lost in our private thoughts. And our private fears.

The people at the hotel knew us by then, of course. They were always very friendly and had regarded us for a long time as "regulars," but they had also learned quickly that we didn't care to talk about where we went on Saturdays. I guess we looked especially tense that day because I remember that the woman just handed us our keys without saying a word. We had our regular rooms by then that they always kept ready for us on Friday. After we'd been going there a while, they had asked me one time if we'd be coming every weekend and I said yes and they gave us a special reduced rate. They're really good, generous people, decent people, and they have no idea of the danger that threatens them. It's because of people like them that we do what we do. It's the thought of people like them that gives us the strength and courage we need.

We ate dinner that night in the hotel's dining room—it's called the Dining Room—and nobody spoke and I remember that it was very quiet because very few people go out to eat on Good Friday. We all ordered a good meal too, trying to build up our strength, I guess, although I'm sure the others had no better appetite for it than I did.

But we forced ourselves to eat and when we were done we went upstairs. Paul and Susanne went off to their room and

Barbara and I went into ours without saying a word to them. None of us could talk, not about anything.

We didn't get much sleep. I stared at the ceiling most of the night and I know that Barbara tossed and turned beside me. I'm sure I must have dozed for a while but I think I was awake more than I was asleep. In the morning, Paul and Susanne looked tired and haggard too.

We didn't say a word as we got into the car and drove out to the woods to meet the old man. There was nothing to say.

It was different this time. Very different.

The old man said nothing, just brought us into the house. The sharpened stakes we had prepared the previous week were lined up against the wall. We shivered at the sight of them. It had been raining and chilly when we left the hotel and drove out to the trail to meet the old man, and that had us shivering too. I guess we wouldn't have given much for our chances just then.

The old man was obviously nervous himself. He couldn't keep his eyes away from the stakes against the wall, kept glancing at them, as if to reassure himself that they were still there. But he knew how we felt too and soon told us that we should get some rest, get as much sleep during the day as we could, because we would have to be out in the woods during the night, before the first light of dawn, and we knew what lay ahead of us.

Without any further talking, we lay down on the rugs and fell instantly asleep.

* * *

He woke us in the night, a little before dawn. I can still feel his bony fingers squeezing my shoulder.

I shivered and saw that the others were just waking up too.

In silence, the old man came to each of us and handed us four of the stakes we'd prepared. When I took mine, the wood felt cold in my hand.

Then we were outside.

The air was wet and cold and we all pulled our jackets tight around us. The old man turned to face us.

"Death to the Easter Bunny!" he whispered. His breath misted in the damp air.

Then he turned and walked slowly but determinedly into the darkest part of the forest, and we followed.

When we had been walking for some minutes, the air seemed to change around us. The mist itself changed and became more like an ordinary thin fog. Then it started raining lightly and we could see a little better, the details of trees and branches becoming clearer as our eyes grew accustomed to the woods. Also, very slowly, the air was getting lighter. The chill and dampness, as well as fear, kept us shivering but we did our best to fight it off. We learned very quickly that you can be frightened and yet be determined to do what you have to do.

We stayed very close together, and very silent, as we made our way through the woods, following the old man.

Finally he stopped and held out a hand as a signal to us. We came up close around him and saw that we were on the edge of a small natural clearing in the woods. Silently, the old man pointed and we could see, in the gradually brightening light, the faintest hint of a trail that entered the clearing on one side and left it on the other. This was where we would wait for the Easter Bunny.

Pointing in silence, the old man indicated where each of us was to hide. Except for the creak of branches overhead, the faint rustle of the pines, and the steady dripping of the rain from the trees, the woods were silent around us in the slowly growing light.

Cold, wet, nervous, we settled down to wait.

It didn't take long.

I was sitting there on the ground, feeling the cold and the rain soaking through my clothes and trying not to think about what was happening. If I stretched my neck up just a little, I could see Barbara in her hiding place a few yards away. I could imagine what was going through her mind right now. She hadn't wanted to believe any of this, hadn't wanted it to be real. None of us did. But of course, we had no choice: the old man spelled it out and when a thing like that is shown to you, you can't just sit back and ignore it. And so here we were. I kept flexing my fingers around the shafts of my four spears. I was afraid that if I sat too still for too long, my fingers would freeze and I'd be at the beast's mercy.

From our hiding places, we could all see the nearly obscure trail that entered at the other side of the clearing. Our eyes were fixed on it as we waited.

And then suddenly I saw something.

Beyond the clearing, some distance away up that barely

visible trail, I thought I saw a movement, thought I saw something white moving between the dark trees. I leaned forward, clutching the spears, and squinted into the fog. I thought I saw it again, something white, whiter than the fog itself, and then instantly it was gone. My heart was pounding, hammering at my chest, and I was short of breath. And then I saw it again.

I stretched upward a little, just enough to see Barbara, and I could tell from the angle and stiffness of her body that she had seen it too.

I held my breath.

And saw it again, closer this time.

It had just been a white blur at first, a patch of whiteness moving against the gray-white of the fog. But now it had a shape. It was upright, and tall. It seemed almost to float or drift between the trees, moving closer and closer to the clearing where we were hiding, but I still couldn't make out any details.

Off to my left, I heard a tiny, stifled choking sound from the old man and then I knew it was really coming.

I closed my eyes for a second, then opened them quickly and focused on the place where I had last seen it. There it was, moving toward us, its shape hidden for a second by the trees, then briefly visible through the thick, swirling fog, then hidden again. The mist and the gray light and my own fear made it appear so large, I thought. It couldn't be as big as it seemed.

It was a rabbit. A huge rabbit. Its thick fur was brilliant white, fuzzy and soft. I could see, as it came slowly closer, its long floppy ears, and thought I could even make out a touch of pink in the insides of them. It had short forepaws, short in relation to its overall size, but huge by any standard, and seemed to be holding them up close to its chest. It wasn't hopping, the way a real rabbit would hop, using its powerful hindquarters, but walking, I could see now, walking purposefully along the trail. There was no mistaking it. It was definitely walking upright in the most grotesque fashion.

I watched it, fascinated and horrified at the same time, as it grew and grew in size and slowly materialized, as it seemed, out of the mist. There was no denying it. I was looking at the Easter Bunny, and everything the old man had said was true.

It was real and unreal at the same time, a thing that moved in this world, the real world, and yet was not *of* this world. A monster.

It had to be killed.

"Death to the Easter Bunny!" I breathed, and carefully crouched, ready to spring at it. I was tense but no longer afraid. I knew what I had to do.

With some uncanny kind of communication that only takes place in moments of extreme crisis, I knew that the others were moving with me, ready to attack the beast the instant it came within range.

And then it was just beyond the clearing. A few steps would bring it into the open space where we could be on it. And, my God, it was enormous, perhaps twice my own height. I could see it now, see it really clearly for the first time. I could see its face, its pink nose, its horribly long white whiskers. And I could see what it was carrying in those paws it held up in front of it. There, brightly decorated with yellow and purple satin ribbons, was a woven straw Easter basket. I had to force myself from freezing at the sight.

The thing stepped into the clearing, almost filling it with its huge size.

And we were on it.

The old man was first. With a hoarse, wordless cry, he sprang from the trees right beside the Easter Bunny, leaped at it, and plunged a spear into the soft white fur of its neck. Taken by surprise, the Easter Bunny reeled back.

The other four of us were already moving, our spears aimed at the thing's heart, as the old man had taught us. I don't know if the others' spears struck home on that first mad thrust, but I know mine did. I felt it strike, felt it sink into resisting flesh. Knowing it was in, I whirled away—the old man had taught us well—and took another of my spears and moved in again to jab at it. The technique was like that of the bull ring: get the first spears in to stick there and weaken and hamper the beast, then go at it with the rest of the spears. I saw blood staining the white fur bright red. Through it all, the beast never made a sound.

Now I could see the other spears in it, dangling from it, whipping around as the Bunny whirled, still confused from the sudden attack. There were several streams of red running through its fur. It was still desperately clutching the Easter basket to its chest, perhaps for protection from the thrusting spears, but that gave us yet another moment of advantage and we made good use of it. One of the flying spears—I think it was one of the old man's—struck it in the face and then one of its eyes was bleeding.

It let go of the basket and whirled around, dropping to all fours and desperately seeking a direction where it could spring to safety. Its mouth was open and blood-flecked foam sprayed out. Its pink eyes darted all around. But we were at it, spears jabbing, thrusting, from every direction, offering it no chance to escape.

The old man was closest in to the beast, almost on top of it, pounding and pounding with his spear. When the one he was using stuck in the monster's side and broke off, he used the remaining piece to poke at its eyes, drawing more blood. The thing crouched lower to the ground, turned, turned back, but we gave it no room to move. It was weakening now, and covered with blood. Then suddenly it rose up on its hindquarters, those powerfully muscled legs that could break a man's back with one kick. If it had a chance to give a single strong thrust, it might get away from us. I saw Paul dash in and drive his spear deep into the thing's belly. Barbara and Susanne were thrusting their points repeatedly at its face and it tried to raise those short forepaws up to protect itself and that's when the old man saw his opening and got in very close, almost directly under the thing where he could have been crushed if it had come down on him, and, using both hands for more power, drove the shaft of his spear directly into the monster's heart and sank it in right up to the place where he held it.

The thing shuddered violently, then was still for an instant, as if delicately balanced. Half a dozen spears protruded from its body. Brilliant red blood stained its white fur. Both eyes were bloody and sightless. The straw basket was trampled and shattered in the mud beneath its enormous feet. We leaped out of the way as it toppled over. The sound it made when it hit the ground seemed loud enough to shake the very floor of the forest and the bedrock of the mountain beneath.

We stood there, sweating, trembling, gasping for air, spears ready, prepared to leap at it again if a single muscle moved or even twitched.

We waited a long time, breathing hard, standing in a circle around its bleeding body, watching its blood soak into the earth, but the Easter Bunny never stirred again.

The four of us live in Deacons Kill now.

We finished out the school term in New York, but didn't sign contracts for another year. We all found jobs in the Kill and work here now. It doesn't really matter what we do, as long as we can support ourselves, and, besides, we live very simply. When we pooled all of our savings, we had enough to buy a house right on the edge of the old man's woods. The four of us live together here and we get along just fine.

Barbara and I were married in June. Susanne wanted to be a June bride too, so we made it a double ceremony. It's good to have friends you can count on, and to be close to them.

And of course we see the old man all the time now.

It's a nice house. It's small but we've made it very comfortable. The nicest part of it, we all agree, is the big fireplace. Once the weather got cool in October, we really appreciated it. None of us minded chopping firewood at all, because it's been so nice to keep a big fire roaring there in the evenings and keeping us warm at night.

But there's no fire in the fireplace tonight. Winters are very cold in the mountains and it's pretty cold in the house right now and the five of us are bundled up to keep warm. But we don't mind. We'll do what we have to do and we'll wait here in the cold and the dark as long as we have to.

Our work was only just started last April when we killed the Easter Bunny. That was only the beginning. Now we have more work to do, and we'll wait here as long as necessary by the fireplace and the chimney, because tonight is the night before Christmas and our stockings are hung and we're ready.

WE HAVE ALWAYS LIVED
IN THE FOREST

Nancy Holder

Brittle Bones, aching joints. I hate growing old. And these children of mine make life less than simple, though that is why we have always lived in the forest.

But you know the young: they never listen to you; at least, mine never do. They struggle and thrash and escape at the first opportunity, thinking they can outrun me—pity's sake, I'm not *that* old!

But not to fear, I always catch them and bring them back. I'm a good mother.

But they try me, they do. Just yesterday, one of my older ones, Victoria, made the break while I was dressing her for dinner. (Such a lovely creature, all in white lace like a bride, a velvet ribbon at her throat.) Just as I was stitching up the back of her gown, she whirled around, shoved me to the floor, and took off shrieking.

The young. So restless and foolish. At least, mine are.

After I regained my balance I watched her for a moment, lace flying as she stumbled and panted, calling to her brothers and sisters to follow—but they stayed where they were, my good darlings. (Besides, I build my fences high.) A few began to cry, others to shout encouragement—*that* will have to be dealt with, no egging on the deserters—but no one joined her.

I thought, Let her go. Let her see what lies beyond the forest. If she won't listen to my warnings, she deserves what she gets.

But I couldn't bear the thought of stumbling on her one day, after they finished with her—the agony would far outweigh the satisfaction.

We have always lived in the forest to enjoy the simple life. And to hide from the town, of course.

After a stern warning to the others, I ran after Victoria; and for a while I thought she was going to make it. I had bruised my hip on the hard dirt floor and my pain slowed my progress. My girl fairly flew among the trees—I couldn't help the pride that surged through me at the sight of her, so beautiful and lithe, ducking heavy oak branches and bearded webs of Spanish moss. She led me a merry dance, though I called to her that she was going too far, getting too deep; the town waited with its maw wide open, slathering its lips to devour her. I believe tears came to my eyes—I care for all my children, though I have so many— and I reached out for her, clutching my sore hip, not at all angry with her for pushing me. For I understand the young, you see.

A good mother always understands.

We raced into the bowels of the forest; despite my concern for Victoria, I shuddered and considered turning back. It was too dank and shadowy, too like my image of the town. But I pressed on into the bracken, so dense and thick my perspiration iced my skin.

I tired; I'm growing old, you see, and they take bigger chances than before; and all seemed lost. My, how she flew, my little gazelle! What a girl she was!

We raced on. The ground grew damp and my feet sank into it, but it caught Victoria, too, and I knew I still had a chance.

She stumbled over a large exposed root and pitched forward into the mud. Even then, she was not daunted—she crawled on her hands and knees, screaming for help. I wanted to ask her who she thought would come. There was no one but us and the town, and she surely didn't want Them to hear her.

But that was my Victoria: looking before she leapt— literally! I almost laughed aloud as I realized the aptness of the phrase, but poor Victoria still pitched forward, positively hysterical. She was almost naked; her dress had caught on the thorns and brambles and ripped in long pieces like bandages, and blood-soaked they were, too, with streaks from her scratches. Her thighs looked like ribbon candy.

"Oh, Vicky," I said sadly, and then I caught her. I embraced her like a huge mother bear, my breast heaving upon hers, and I scooped her up in my arms as if she were an infant.

She was beyond struggling; she hung limply in my arms, begging, "No, Mother, no. Please, not me."

"You've been very silly," I told her. "What did you expect to accomplish?"

"Oh, please, Mother," and suchlike. I have often told them not to whine. It is distasteful in a young person.

Halfway back, she rallied and tried to escape again, but I held her tightly (and gave her a tap on the chin, I must admit, though not too hard).

Now all the children were crying, a few on their knees, sobbing out my errant daughter's name. She held out a limp arm to them, staring over my shoulder as I carried her into the house.

I bathed my darling girl, in the big tin tub by the fireplace. She had exhausted herself, for which I was grateful—I was tired, too, and she might have been able to make it if she rallied herself one last time.

The others kept up their wailing, even after the sun set. I lit some candles and eased Victoria out of the tub, dried her, and patiently dressed her again, this time in scarlet to blend in with her wounds.

And then I ate her. She was as delicate and sweet as I had imagined, and I felt proud of her all over again.

In the forest we lived a simple, self-sufficient life, and I protect my children from the horrors of the town. You would think they'd understand, and stop fighting me, but that's not the way of children, is it? Has it ever been? One can only sigh over their ignorance and do one's best.

In the forest, at least, it is easier. I can't bear to think what happens to those of the town.

As, still, I can scarcely bring myself to think about the poor thing who dragged herself here shortly after I devoured Victoria.

I sensed her presence before I saw her. I knew there was a stranger near, and though my hip ached and my meal made me sluggish, I roused myself from the warmth of the fire and staggered across the room.

I heard footsteps, and for one awful instant, I thought we were in terrible danger. I fumbled behind the door for my club and tiptoed out the back to the pens, warning my girls and boys to be quiet; which, in the contrary ways of children, made them shout the louder—oh, children! Sometimes I wish—but no, that's cruel. I wouldn't have life any other way.

I made my way back from the pen to the house and stood behind the locked front door, club at the ready. But what can you do against one of Them? They're practically invincible; I've never heard of a death among Them. Of course, we live far away and I know little of Their ways except Their savagery; perhaps one day my ignorance will prove my undoing, but in this case, I was fortunate.

After a murmured prayer I crept to the window and pulled back the curtain just a little, steeling myself for what must surely be the messengers of a grizzly, torturous death.

To my delight, a small girl leaned against the door, head bowed, panting. (I couldn't hear her, of course, for the screaming of my own children; but I saw her red face and her bony shoulders convulsing.)

Now I'm sure you know that many would have sent her on her way; but as I stared at her my maternal instinct rose in my breast like a flame, and I knew I had to help. Without a second thought—for she could have been part of a trap—I opened the door.

She saw me and flung herself into my arms. "Oh, help us!" she cried, and collapsed.

Poor little waif, her feet were pulp. I lay her on my bed and bathed her; in her sleep, she flinched when I touched her. She was in worse shape than Victoria had been, and I knew without a doubt she had escaped from town.

It chilled me. This lovely child, at Their hands—

I was so upset I was sick. I lost my dinner in the same spot behind the house I go to periodically—that's another trial of growing old, that one has trouble digesting now and then—and when I came back, the dear creature was sitting up and clutching my quilt to her chest. Her eyes were huge and filled with tears.

"Where's my mother?" she asked when I came into the room.

I didn't know what to say, but I was saved from answering by a soft thumping on the door.

"Mama!" the child cried, though I shushed her, and "Angel!" a desperate voice carried through the heavy door.

When I opened it, a gaunt, pale woman fell at my feet.

"Take me, take me," she murmured. "Only spare the child."

Her words confused me, but I helped her onto the bed beside her little one and urged her to rest.

"You're safe here," I assured her, but she shook her head.

"Nowhere is safe."

"But you're in the forest."

"Nowhere is safe," she repeated, and fainted.

They slept for an entire day and night. Both had fevers

and I placed cool cloths on their foreheads, but they appeared to grow worse.

I lit my big stove and made them some gruel from my newest, little Jamie. He was most compliant, though he cried at the end. Silly boy. I shall miss him.

I fed the gruel to the mother and child, but they spit it all back up. I gave them bread, and they managed to keep that down, and some water, which I have little of, and all that seemed to have some effect. So I tried the gruel again, with no luck. It seemed to make them sicker.

Then the mother awoke with a start; her feverish gaze searched the room until it fell on me, and I smiled, saying, "Don't you remember me?"

"The kind old lady." She sighed and put her hand to the forehead of her child. "She's burning up."

"I gave you some gruel, but it didn't seem to agree with you," I told her. "Maybe you should try again."

"You're most generous."

"Not at all."

She accepted a bowl from me and looked at me with big, brown eyes that melted my heart. In the forest, there are no visitors. I don't believe I had ever seen another grown person in my life. Of course, I'm getting old now, and they say one's memory begins to slip. Why, I couldn't even remember all the names of my children. But then, there have been so many.

She looked strange as she drank the gruel, but finished the bowl and handed it back to me.

"If you don't mind, may I have some for my daughter?"

"Of course."

I began to ladle some into the bowl, but the woman became violently ill, vomiting everything back up on my granny-stitch quilt.

"Oh, I'm sorry. I'm so sorry," she said, weeping. "What shall I do? I'm sure They're following us."

I finished wiping her off and sat beside her on the bed. "Just rest. It will be safe. It's safe in the forest."

But I wasn't at all sure of that. If she were right, and They were following her, They would punish me for harboring her. And my children, oh, Lord, what would They do to them? I couldn't eat all of them. Yet if I hid them, they would be sure to start their caterwauling, not understanding the situation at all—which I wouldn't expect them to, they're just children.

You can certainly understand my dilemma.

She slept fitfully after that, and I wished there were something I could do. I had a bowl of gruel—it was tasty, of course; Jamie was a good little boy—and sat by the window, looking for the first sign of Them.

I awakened in the morning. I had dozed in the chair all night. My bones were stiff and I knew that, if any of my children tried to escape that day, I would probably be unable to stop them, unless they were tiny infants.

The woman jerked awake and began dressing herself and whispering to her child.

"May we have some water, please?" she asked. "And then we'll be on our way."

I didn't begrudge her the cup, but it worried me—I use so much with my gruels and stews and such, and my supply was growing low—and then she asked me for a second, for the girl.

"Is she better today?" I asked.

The woman felt the brave little forehead. "I think so. She seems cooler."

I touched her myself. "The fever's completely gone," I told her, surprised she couldn't discern it. Then I felt her own skin. It was as hot as the inside of my oven.

"I'm sick, aren't I?" the woman wailed. "Oh, poor Angel, what shall we do?"

I have never been one to offer advice unless it's asked for, but this poor lady was dreadfully in need of some clear thinking.

I took both her hands in mine and said, "My dear, it's obvious that the child is well enough. Mine apparently aren't agreeing with you."

She looked puzzled.

"It's time to eat her."

You would have thought I'd told her to set the house on fire.

She backed away from me on the bed, nearly trampling the child, who cried out, and scrabbled into the corner.

"Do *what?*" She cried. "What?"

"You must have nourishment if you're to survive," I said, quite reasonably. "My children are making you sick."

She stared at me for a long time, her eyes so big I was afraid they might fall out. Then she stared down at her stomach and let out the most bloodcurdling scream. My children must have heard it, for they answered in kind, ringing my eardrums. (I have since made myself a charming set of earmuffs, which I wear when they are in their moods.)

"I've been eating your . . . ?" She didn't say any more, only fell to crying and screaming and thrashing around. I was afraid she had gone mad from her high temperature.

And then she spied her little one, who had awakened (naturally; not even the dead could have slept through her hysteria), and she clasped the girl to her breast. The child struggled, then grew still, and I thought for a moment the woman had taken my advice and smothered her.

But she crawled off the bed, her child clinging to her like a baby monkey, and fell to the floor. She pitched herself forward to the door, and I was so reminded of Victoria that I smiled across the room at her shredded white dress, which I planned to wash and repair so my other girls could wear it.

"Oh, my god, my god," she muttered, over and over, flailing at the doorknob. "My god, she's crazy."

"If you want to leave, you have but to ask," I said. Naturally, I was confused, and a little affronted as well. I had offered this stranger the comfort and sanctuary of my home, and in return she insulted me. I was of a mind to point out that *she* was the one going off her head, not I; and so just who was the madwoman around here?

But I have been well brought up, and I reminded myself that she was quite ill; so I turned the knob and opened the door.

She slithered out on her knees, dropping and gathering up her child, throwing her head back and yowling.

My children, as you can imagine, were in such a state I knew there would never be any peace again.

The woman staggered to her feet and quit my door, then looked at the tall wooden boards of the pen.

"And is that where you keep them?" she screamed. "Your

children? You herd them like animals?"

"Mercy, no, they're children," I said carefully, for I knew now that she had indeed gone insane. It was as if she didn't hear my wee ones, though their pleas were deafening. I had to bellow like an ox to make her hear me.

"God, god," she moaned, and lifted the latch.

It was as if that motion waved black fortune into the forest.

For on the horizon, I saw the devil carriages of the town; and I knew inside They would ride, in Their black cloaks and hoods, with Their knives and hooks and syringes. With a wail of despair, I knew all my care was for nothing. My darlings were in mortal peril.

"We must all run," I cried, "but first help me eat the little ones, oh, do; it will go cruelest for them."

She burst into tears. I think she meant to hide herself and her daughter in the pen, for she threw open the gate and jumped inside; and then, though the death coaches were lunging ever closer, she shrieked with horror and gestured to my babes.

Her entire body shook. Her child tugged at her skirts, crying, "Mama! Let's go! Please!" but the woman only trembled.

Then she began to laugh. It was frenzied, awful laughter, and she pointed at me and said, "Your children are made of mud! You've made little statues to amuse yourself!"

She was clearly beyond reason, but I simply could not abandon her.

"Quickly, before They come, eat her. You know it is your duty."

She couldn't stop laughing. "Is that what you did?" she asked me, and her voice was high-pitched like a maniac's.

"We must go," I warned her.

But it was too late. The devil carriages swooped down on us and They clambered out, full of fury and evil, and the woman collected herself just as They stormed the pen.

"What have I done?" she cried. "I have failed my Angel!" She fell on her knees before Them, arms outstretched.

"Take me," she whispered, but the tallest of Them replied, "You know it is not you we want."

Their knives flashed. Their teeth sparkled behind Their masks. I saw the hooks of Their hands and the heavy boots, made for grinding little bones.

They seemed to pay no attention to me, almost to pretend I wasn't there. I darted around the leader and whispered to the woman:

"My oven is lit. Better to toss the girl in than—"

But the leader heard me. He took a menacing step toward the woman and said, "You know it is too late. We will not be cheated."

I turned to my children. "It is your turn to do a good deed! Eat her!"

But they cowered and ran the other way. Who can blame them? They are only children.

Eventually, of course, They tore the girl away from the mother, though she held on as if her own life depended on it. In fact, They hacked her out of her arms, carving great, gaping chunks of flesh from her bones and breaking her fingers. Had I not looked after her, she would have died. But she mended, though she lost use of most of her fingers.

And one night, while I was asleep, she left. A note beside

my cooking pot read, "Gone to Town. I am too lonely here. I miss
. . . almost everything."

I was most distraught, for I had grown to care for the dear mad thing, but perhaps she would be happier there.

As for me, I prefer my own company, and that of my children.

Which is why we have always lived in the forest.

PROLOGUE: AS THE WOLF
LOVES WINTER

David Poyer

What follows is the prologue to David Poyer's mysterious and frightening novel As the Wolf Loves Winter, *in which wolves restake their claim to a remote section of Pennsylvania.*

The man in the rust-colored parka had almost reached the crest of the mountain, after a long, wearying climb, when he first suspected he wasn't alone.

He stopped, thrusting thumbs under pack straps as he frowned around at the monotonous gray trees. The blowing snow made them wavering and grainy, like an old film. Something had moved out there. But what? He's left the last house, the last road miles back. The only trails up here were deer trails. Hunters? But the season was over, and few hunters came back this far anyway.

Around the listening figure the hills rose steep as the waves of a frozen sea storm. Till now in his march he'd looked up at them. Now he stood on the ridgeline, knowing there was only a little way yet to the summit. The long crests shouldered forward under snow that hissed steadily down from clouds the color of a worn spoon. In the afternoon light no road or building, no human artifice or habitation was visible on the deserted land.

Finally he decided it must have been a deer. But cold and fatigue had stiffened his muscles during the pause, and he winced as he forced them into motion again. The deep unbroken snow dragged at his boots. Dropping his head, he bulled along through heavier drifts where the woods opened, then into a stand of white pines. Their resinous smell stung his nose pleasantly.

Yeah, getting tired . . . he was still in good shape, though. Not like the other guys at work. He couldn't think of one who could have kept up with him out here. He smiled faintly, planting one foot ahead of the other as the ridgeline lifted toward the clouds. New snow creaked and popped under his boots. From time to time he looked up.

At last he glimpsed a wedge of sky between the stripped boles. He stopped again, blowing out with relief, and shrugged the pack higher on his shoulders. Light when he'd left the car, it had gained an astonishing amount of weight as he'd humped it across miles of forest and up nearly a thousand feet to this deserted height.

His eyes searched the trees, the hundreds of stark vertical lines with snow sifting and whirling between them. No wonder they called it the Wild Area. The vacant, wind-ringing woods, the mist-wreathed hollows didn't feel empty. They felt haunted. He didn't believe in ghosts or spirits. But it was spooky out here. Wild, like the forest of fairy tales, or of nightmare.

The Kinningmahontawany, they called it.

He shifted the pack again, then bent for the last time to the slope. Around him the oaks stretched skeletal limbs in impotent entreaty to an indifferent heaven, the colorlessness broken only occasionally on the misty hill flanks by the bluegreen of pine. That might have been what I saw, he thought. An evergreen bough collapsing, giving way at last under its icy and ever-increasing burden.

A labyrinthine writhe of blown-down trunks and shattered limbs opened above him. Years before a wind had swept up from the hollow, or a tornado had touched down. Beneath the fallen trees holes opened like black mouths ringed with jagged bark teeth. The snow supported his weight at first, then gave way with a sullen, treacherous crackle, plunging him thigh-deep, filling his boots and pockets with icy powder.

When he emerged from the blowdown, soaked with sweat under the parka, the ground leveled out. It wasn't easy to know when you were at the top. There was no open vista to look out from. But as he slogged on, the land started to drop. He stopped, resting, then backtracked.

At last he judged he was as near the summit of Colley Hill as he was likely to get without surveyor's instruments. He didn't have to find the exact apex, but the closer he got the more even the repeater's coverage would be. Coughing white breath like cigarette smoke into the icy wind, he unslung the pack. Digging a gloved hand into his aching neck, he peered up into dully glowing clouds, murky and turbulent, but at their hearts the same dead gray as the motionless trunks around him.

Finally he decided on a huge old black cherry. Like an ancient column, it towered straight-trunked up at the crown of the hill. Its upper limbs were twisted, lightning-shattered, but it looked like it would be here for years to come. He knelt to the pack and unzipped it, revealing a coil of insulated wire, a foot-square panel, and a plastic case sealed with epoxy. He set these aside and pulled out a set of climbing spikes and a lineman's belt.

Straightening, he peered around once again, still wondering what that movement had been. Like a ghost slipping through the empty woods, among the winterstripped trees . . .

He clamped the spikes onto his boots, shrugged off the parka—this would be warm work—and draped it over ice-brittled laurel. Tucking box and wire inside his sweater, he pulled on heavy leather gloves, looking up.

A few minutes later he was sixty feet up, stapled and strapped to the black pillar of the ancient cherry. Even through the gloves he felt the dead, sapless cold of the sleeping wood. The wind was much worse up here. Unslowed by underbrush or second growth, it scraped the hilltops like a knife across a cutting board, laying icy steel against his cheeks and ears.

He climbed rapidly, setting the spikes with his toes, then levering himself upward against the huge rough cylinder that narrowed as he rose. From time to time he came to branches, massive outstretched shoulders, and had to unbuckle the belt and work his way over them. Some were cracked from ice load and lightning storm. At these moments, with only the strength of his arms holding him, he couldn't help thinking all he had to do was open his hands . . . and some obscure part of him that stepped out of the shadows only at times like these urged him to: to let go, fall, and die. The only way he could keep going was to close his mind against it, as a man looks away from fear, or madness, or unpermitted desire; things that once acknowledged are half surrendered to.

Twenty feet from the crown of the tree he paused for a rest. He tugged at the belt, making sure it was locked, then leaned back and clamped a glove over his face. As his breath warmed his cheeks, wasp-stinging them back to life, he looked out over an immense and lifeless solitude.

From up here, high above the summit, hundreds of square miles of hills stretched out like sleeping cats beneath the falling snow. The bellies of the clouds dragged on the prickly tops of the ridges, the dead-looking branches snagging tufts of white fog like wool and combing it out to lie in opaque drifts in the benches and hollows. Everything was black, and gray, and white; a world possessed by winter so profoundly it seemed impossible that anything could ever change.

White, and gray, and black . . . and a furtive stir at the periphery of vision.

He whipped his head around, peering down through the treetops like a bird of prey. But his eyes were not a hawk's eyes, and again his focused sight found nothing. Nothing but the snow, and the slowly vanishing connect-the-dots of his own trail, ending far below.

Puffing out a stream of frost-smoke, he set his spikes again and hoisted himself to where he could wrap one arm around the narrowed trunk. The great tree soared upward still. But this was as high as he could force himself. Anchoring his weight with a locked elbow, stripping a glove off the other hand with his teeth, he reached inside his sweater.

Checking the lay of the hills, he set the panel so that it would face south and pressed its spiked back into the black bark. He spun the wire out, then swung the box in an arc and let go. It landed on the next branch up. He tensed, clinging to the tree. The box rocked, then dropped over the branch and hung from its antenna.

He smiled, as much as his cold-stiffened face would permit.

He was a radio ham, and the box was an FM relay. Dotted through the countryside, these boxes let hobbyists communicate outside the crowded and sometimes undependable shortwave bands. Powered by the sun, they would serve for years before they had to be replaced.

Huge as it was, the cherry swayed as a gust drove through it. He quickly fumbled his glove back on, afflicted by a shiver both of cold and anxiety. He'd raised four daughters on nursery rhymes, and the repetitive verses played themselves back at odd moments. Rock-a-bye baby, he thought. Daddy better get the hell out of this treetop. If the bough broke, it could be days, maybe weeks, before anybody found him.

He was setting his spikes for the descent when a throaty rumble came from below him.

When he looked down his lips parted in astonishment. What was a German shepherd doing out here? It stood at the base of the tree, staring up at him. He let go with one hand and waved. "Hey, boy," he called, but his voice sounded weak and tremulous against the enormous empty chant of the wind.

The dog went silent for a moment after he spoke. Then the low growl built again, like the sound of a distant battle.

He felt suddenly apprehensive. He tightened his grip on the belt, twisting his spurs into the rough bark, then looked down again, studying the animal.

The first thing he noticed was how long its legs were. The second, the pinkish-red tongue hanging from a black-rimmed mouth. Then, one by one, other details. The brindled coat was the color of wood-smoke, the shoulders and head outlined in charcoal. The pointed ears were forward-focused on him. He was too high to see its eyes. The big splayed paws rested easily on the snow. The fluffed-out tail was carried half lifted as the animal circled the tree, nosing at his pack, then the parka. It had narrow shoulders and a smallish head, and wasn't as big as he'd first thought. Not large for a shepherd, certainly not as big as a Saint Bernard or a rottweiler.

His eyes darted hopefully around, but he saw no sign of its owner. Nor could he make out a collar. It was probably feral. People thought they were being merciful, abandoning their pets in the country. They told themselves they'd make it on their own, but what happened was they starved, or farmers shot them.

Giving the relay a last glance, he began working his way back down the trunk. This occupied his attention for some minutes. Going down was harder than going up. He was shuddering now. The wind's icicle teeth gripped his bunched, straining biceps and thighs. He got to the last branch, twenty feet up, and perched on it to readjust the belt for the final descent. He glanced curiously down again as he did so.

The dog was sitting on its haunches now, still looking at

him. A frosting of fresh snow had gathered on its back. He could see its eyes now. Flat, curiously expressionless, golden orbs that did not look away but stayed locked on his.

Suddenly it lifted its muzzle, opening its mouth in a tremulous, high-pitched wail that echoed and re-echoed, first from the trees, then from the bare, far-off flanks of the hills.

A shiver ran across his shoulders as he heard the answering howls. He clung to the branch and made no further move to come down.

Presently three more forms materialized from the forest. They came one by one, gliding with an easy lope across snow he'd slogged through laboriously. From different directions, as if each had been hunting on its own. As they trotted up each new arrival touched noses with the first, or gave a short, whining bark. They examined the parka, then sniffed and snapped at the pack, pulling it around until the contents lay scattered on the snow. Then they circled restlessly for quite some time, looking up at him with the same speculative stare as the first, before curling themselves into the snow as if it were a down quilt. One shifted several times, unable to find a comfortable spot, till settling on a patch of open snow.

The man clung to the tree, watching them. His arms were shaking now, muscles cramping. The wind came through the cableknit sweater as if it were made of lace. When he lifted his eyes to scan the ice-scoured woods, the snow drove needles into them. When he lowered them to the animals again their gazes met his, unconcerned, opaque, intent, and unafraid.

They can't be, he thought. There aren't any of those left around here. Not for a hundred, two hundred years.

He clapped his arms awkwardly against his chest, sitting crouched over on the icy limb. At the movement heads rose, ears cocked. He explored his pockets. A jackknife, nothing to face four wolves with. A stripping tool. A pair of needlenosed pliers.

He poised the pliers like a pub dart and threw them at the first wolf, still sitting below him. It leapt aside and they missed. It sniffed at the hole in the snow, then followed its tail around and lay down again in the same expectant position as before. He threw the stripping tool too, but it went so wide the animal didn't bother to move. It just sat there, tongue lapping out, looking up at him with what almost seemed to be a grin.

During the next hour he passed from shuddering through numbness to a frozen immobility. Sitting on the limb, buckled to the trunk by the lineman's belt, he didn't need to worry about falling. But he understood now that unless he could build a fire soon, or at least recover the parka, he would die.

He thought of his .22 rifle, at home in the hall closet . . . If he'd brought something to eat, he could toss it to one of the wolves, make them fight over it, maybe get to his parka while they were distracted. But the only food he'd brought was a Hershey bar, and it lay now below him, nosed but undisturbed by the wolves. He thought of cutting off a branch, wiring the knife to it to make a spear. But he couldn't get out to a limb that would break, and when he tried to unbend his fingers from the belt they were frozen to it, like iron clamped to leather. He might uncrimp them, but then he might not be able to close them again.

If he went down, the wolves might kill him. But there

was no question about what the cold would do.

Meanwhile the day dimmed toward darkness, and the snow whispered to him with the tongues of dead leaves. *Soon,* it sounded like. *Soon, soon.*

Finally he decided he had no choice but to try. If he could wound or kill the pack leader, maybe the others would run.

He pried his fingers apart clumsily. His hands still bent, but not as individual fingers. He lobster-clawed the knife open and gripped it in his palm like a Neolithic hand ax. He shifted his feet around toward the tree, dug the spikes in, and reached round to unsnap the belt.

The wolves rose, leaving their comfortable positions and trotting forward to gather beneath him. His heart thudded. Warmth touched his face again, throbbed in his hands. He fixed his eyes on the russet nylon of the parka, judging the number of strides to it. Okay, big bad wolves, he thought with resigned dread. Here I come, ready or not.

Instead he heard a crack, felt a sudden, sagging drop. He whipped around, grabbing for the trunk, but his frozen, scrabbling fingers slipped off. His kicking feet gouged off spinning clods of bark but gained no purchase.

The rotten branch gave another rifle-crack and disintegrated into wood-meal and ice, peeling off a long, splitting strip of bark as it came apart under his weight. The woods spun above his head. The last thing he saw was a gray patchwork of sky.

The wolves stood in a rough circle around the motionless figure sprawled in the snow. Then, into the gathering night, rose a haunting, ululating chorus that the gusting wind carried far out over the darkening hills.

CAUGHT IN THE JAWS
OF DEATH

Jerry MacDonald

"Matthias, come see!" Claudia Garschhammer shouted as she
jumped from the canoe onto shore.

Matthias Ruppert and Claudia, both 26, had been paddling through frigid rain for three hours that day, June 9, 1994.
Now Claudia had spotted a cabin where they could rest up and
get warm. But as they approached, they saw notes on the door
left by earlier paddlers: "Warning: Big black bear. May 13, 1994.
Stole my backpack!" Another message, about a week old: "Bear
tried to steal our packs as we were unloading canoe. We scared
it off by making lots of noise." Resolving to be extra careful, the
two decided to press on to another campsite.

Battling waves and driving rain, Matthias and Claudia
kept paddling. Blond and blue-eyed with an athlete's build,
Matthias shivered as the icy waters of Isaac Lake spilled

over the gunwale and soaked his hiking boots. *Some holiday,* he thought. But he had to admit that Bowron Lake Provincial Park was beautiful. Cold, clear mountain lakes and rugged portages formed a 70-mile chain in British Columbia's Caribbo Mountains, attracting canoeists from around the world. This June day was the third of their planned ten-day trip.

After paddling several more torturous hours, Claudia and Matthias spotted Campsite 21 at Lynx Creek. As the couple turned their canoe toward shore, the wind ceased, the clouds broke and a rainbow arched across the glasslike stillness of the lake. A large bull moose swam by them. It was the Canadian wilderness of picture books, and the canoeists felt a deep contentment.

Matthias and Claudia came from small German towns near the Austrian border. They had met a few months earlier at a hospital in Munich where they both worked. Matthias was a sixth-year medical student with a special interest in emergency/trauma medicine; Claudia, a slender brunette with a warm smile, was a physiotherapist. As their friendship grew, they discovered a mutual excitement for the outdoors—for getting away from the pressures of city life. After Matthias learned he had been accepted for training at Seattle's Harborview Medical Center, he asked Claudia to join him on a Canadian wilderness outing before his tour of duty began.

As they roamed about Campsite 21, Matthias and Claudia saw a small cabin. Two other campers were already there and offered to share space with them. But the German couple preferred to pitch a tent under the open sky. This would be more like the wilderness adventure they'd envisioned.

That evening Claudia celebrated the change in weather by making herb noodles and fresh bread. After dinner, they stowed their food and most of their gear in a "bear cache," a platform strung high between two poles and accessible only by ladder. In the cabin they stored their packsacks containing a first-aid kit and some clothes. They went to sleep that night exhausted but exhilarated.

About six the next morning, when the men in the cabin broke camp, Claudia and Matthias were still asleep. They were awakened as the morning's stillness was broken by a snuffling sound. A large form brushed against their tent. Near the zippered entrance they saw a dark figure moving outside.

Claudia and Matthias sat bolt upright in their sleeping bags. "A bear!" Matthias said under his breath. To frighten the animal off, they began whistling and yelling. When they stopped, they could hear only their own panicked breathing. Had the intruder left?

Suddenly the bear's claws came ripping through the tent. "Get under your mattress—quick!" Matthias yelled. He pushed Claudia down and threw her foam pad over her. He scrambled to get under his own pad, but it was too late. The tent collapsed as the bear pounced. Matthias was pinned by the 275-pound creature.

Play dead, he thought. This had been the advice of hiking guide-books he'd read. But an instant later the bear raked its claws across Matthias's back and legs, sending a searing flash of pain through him. Next it began to bite and tear chunks of flesh from Matthias's left buttock and hip. Trapped under the wreckage of the tent, Claudia could only listen helplessly to Matthias's screams. When she spied a small hole in the tent above her head, she thrust her fingers through and ripped the fabric. Pushing her head out, she found herself face to face with the bear, blood dripping from its jaws. Matthias called out, "Claudia, help! It's killing me."

As the savagery of the attack increased, Matthias felt his mind becoming strangely detached. The medical student found himself analyzing his injuries as if they were someone else's. *The bear must have hit the sciatic nerve,* he thought when a bite sent pain through his body and numbed his left leg.

Claudia realized that if Matthias was to live, she had to do something. *I must stay calm,* she repeated to herself. Moving slowly, keeping out of the bear's sight, she crawled from the tent, stood up and sprinted the 30 feet to the cabin.

I'm going to die, Matthias thought. Then he realized with horror that the bear could continue attacking him without killing him if no arteries were cut. *Let the agony end,* he pleaded silently. *If only I could lose consciousness.* An image flashed before him of his mother in Germany. Matthias was an only child, and he feared his mother would never get over his death.

Her heart pounding, Claudia scanned the inside of the cabin. There, next to one of the packsacks, lay a 12-inch wood-handled hatchet. She grabbed it and ran out the door as Matthias gave another agonized scream. Thrashing about, he had managed to get his head out from under the tent. Instantly the bear lunged and sank its inch-long canines into the side of Matthias's skull. With its jaws clamped, the bear yanked him upward, trying to free him from the tent. Its teeth scraped along Matthias's scalp, peeling the skin away.

Claudia moved behind the bear and crept closer. Less than an arm's length away, tensing her body, she swung the hatchet at the back of the bear's neck. Stunned, the animal dropped its victim and headed into the forest.

Matthias, on the ground, was covered in blood and barely conscious. "You must walk!" Claudia urged. "Quick, before the bear returns!"

"I can't get up," he replied weakly.

Still clutching the hatchet, Claudia put Matthias's arm around her neck and dragged him to the cabin. Once inside, he collapsed on the floor, bleeding from puncture wounds all over his body. A gaping hole marked his left buttock. Half his scalp was peeled back. "What should I do, Matthias?" Claudia pleaded.

Concentrate! he told himself. *React calmly and you have a chance.* "Get the first-aid kit and thermal blanket in the pack-sack," Matthias said. He knew he had a better chance of surviving if he stayed warm. "Don't bother with my head wounds. The others are more serious." Then he told Claudia to bandage his bleeding leg and buttock.

Following Matthias's instructions, Claudia positioned him on the cabin floor so that if he lost consciousness and vomited, he wouldn't choke to death. As Claudia wrapped him in the blanket, he told her what she already knew. She'd have to go for help alone.

But first, Matthias realized, he needed water from the

lake to prevent dehydration. Claudia opened the door to get some—then slammed it.

"It's back!" she said, her face going white. The bear was standing over the tent, nosing at the blood-soaked nylon.

"Don't go out," Matthias ordered. "It's too dangerous."

Claudia knew Matthias needed help right away. She grabbed the hatchet and a piece of firewood and stepped onto the porch. She screamed at the animal, waving the weapon and heaving the wood. The bear retreated to the forest. Now Claudia sprinted to the lake to fill a metal canteen. When she returned, she built a fire in the potbellied stove. "If the bear comes, you must fight for your life!" she said and pressed the hatchet into Matthias's hand.

Opening the door a crack, Claudia peered out: the bear was back. Once more she screamed and threw wood; again the animal retreated. Claudia latched the door behind her and secured it with rope. Then she raced to the lake, jumped into the canoe and set off for the ranger cabin over seven miles away. The craft zigzagged in the water; it was her first time paddling alone. Blisters on her hands broke open. She blocked out the pain and pressed on. Hoping to attract campers, she stayed close to shore, screaming for help. Nobody answered.

Matthias drifted in and out of consciousness. Suddenly he heard a scratching sound. He turned to the window six feet away and gasped. Standing on its haunches and scraping at the metal screen was the bear. Attracted by the smell of Matthias's blood, the animal had come back. With one swipe, it could rip the screen and crawl inside.

Okay, Matthias thought, *I'll show you I can still fight!* He got to his feet. Gripping the hatchet, he took one step toward the window and collapsed on the floor.

Shifting his weight to his good leg, he pulled himself back up. Gathering strength, he let out a roar of rage and pain and threw himself across the room at the window. He managed to swing the hatchet at the sill in front of the bear's face.

Had he hit it? He couldn't tell. But the last thing he saw before losing consciousness was the animal lumbering toward the woods. When Matthias came to, he realized the bear could return at any moment, so he struggled to secure the shutters on the windows. Then, crawling across the floor, he shoved the wooden table toward the door and lay beside the stove, utterly spent, in a pool of his own blood.

As his body grew colder, Matthias thought about his future, about graduating from medical school, about a recipe for his favorite bread—anything to stay conscious. He tried not to think of the bear, but he couldn't help himself. *An animal of such strength could surely break down the front door of the cabin if it wanted to.*

It was 10:15 A.M. Claudia had been gone over 2½ hours. Matthias willed himself not to panic. There was no telling how long it would be before she could return with help. If she had to go all the way back to the park entrance, he reasoned, it might take days. Already he was frighteningly short of breath. How long could he hang on?

Around 10:30, near the northern end of Isaac Lake, Claudia spotted a ranger boat. She waved frantically, and a few moments later Reg Plett and Damaris Kunzler pulled alongside. Claudia wept as she told them about Matthias.

At first Plett and Kunzler couldn't quite believe their ears—there hadn't been a bear mauling reported in the more than 30 years the park had been open. With their boat at full throttle, Plett radioed for a helicopter to be on standby.

At 10:55, four hours after the attack, the ranger boat arrived at Campsite 21. Keeping a sharp lookout for the bear, the three rushed to the cabin. "Matthias!" Claudia shouted. "We're here!" No answer.

"Matthias! Answer me!" Claudia pleaded, putting her shoulder to the door and pushing hard. Finally it gave way. From the darkness a weak voice muttered, "Who's there?" Claudia rushed to Matthias and, lightly touching his face, whispered everything would be okay.

About eight hours after the attack, Matthias Ruppert was wheeled into surgery at G. R. Baker Memorial Hospital in Quesnel, 75 miles away. For two hours surgeons worked to sew up the damage the bear had inflicted. It took 200 stitches to close the wounds in Matthias's face, neck, arms, leg and buttock. No vital organs had been damaged, but he had come within an hour of bleeding to death. He was just regaining consciousness when Claudia came to his bedside. "Thank you for saving my life," she said softly. "Thank you for saving mine," Matthias replied.

Two days after the attack, ranger Reg Plett destroyed an eight-year-old black bear snared near the cabin at Lynx Creek. With no sign of other bear activity in the area then and for days afterward, park officials are confident they caught the right bear.

Matthias Ruppert was transferred to Harborview Medical Center in Seattle, where he spent seven weeks undergoing surgery and recuperating. By September, he was well enough to begin his training. Today he still limps and has panic attacks recalling that day last June. But the event left another legacy as well. "I feel more for my patients, their fright and their pain," he says. "I hope I carry that through the rest of my life."

SWAMP

SURVIVAL EXERCISE

Talmage Powell

To: CAPT. L. G. McCabe, Intelligence Officer

5th Bn., 22nd Marines, Parris Island, S.C.

Sir: In the event that I can't appear in person for debriefing re Survival Exercise to which I, Master Sergeant James C. Kelly, and Privates Rodney Gordon and Sidney Finklestein were assigned, I offer the following informal report.

This may be the only means of making known the events that began at Point E. I feel that my chances are good of returning to Point E, if only temporarily. If I must abandon the location or fail to survive, the report will be there, awaiting the helicopter scheduled to pick up the Survival Exercise team.

As you know, it was to be a routine exercise to provide experience in living off the land, as would a small unit isolated in enemy territory.

Enemy territory is hardly the phrase to describe the locale in which the team composed of Gordon, Finklestein, and I found ourselves. We stepped from the normal into a delirium in which survival became a mockery—and if you find this report beyond belief I would remind you, sir, that I have no reason for deceit and am testifying on my honor as a United States Marine.

Ferried in by helicopter, the team was in top form, even by Marine standards. Young, tough, battle-ready, Finklestein and Gordon regarded the week-long exercise as an adventuresome break in base camp routine. They fully expected to be cracking an icy beer eight days from now and telling their buddies what it was like, going into a tropical wilderness without supplies, equipped only with trench knives at their waists and matches in their pockets.

In my own case, I had been on one previous Survival Exercise, in Alaska, and I felt the coming week would be something of a camp out. After all, Florida was my native state. Even though I had never set foot in the deep interior of the Everglades, I had fished the murmuring bayous and hunted the pine forests before they were overcome by condominiums, retirement cities, expressways, Disney Worlds, and Big Mac wrappers. As a rural boy I had rubbed shoulders with Seminoles. Later, during my two years at Florida State, a Seminole had been one of my closest friends. I knew the Indian legends and lore, the basics for living bare-handedly off the lush land. You would think, Captain McCabe, that I was going into a classroom with the quiz answers up my sleeve.

But as the helicopter whirred us deeper into the 'Glades, I was reminded that it wasn't all going to be crabcakes and beer.

Beyond the horizon the familiar planet had vanished. The uninhabited reaches overwhelmed our senses as we stared down through the Plexiglas bubble. We looked out over the limitless sweep of a watery jungle unlike any other on earth, a sun-broiled morass that could swallow the state of Rhode Island almost four times over. It was a world of molten sun reflections from shallow water, or razor-sharp sawgrass and small, low islands—hummocks—scattered wherever vegetation had reared up and rotted for a million years. It was strands of cypress older than the Crusades, burdened with heavy gray curtains of Spanish moss, providing life for the enormous, parasitic, obscenely hued wild orchids strung along the tall trunks. It was a seething incubator where mists and vapors slithered and the nights crashed and roared in the eternal struggle for survival. It was alligator, and poisonous vipers, and puma on the prowl, and stalk-legged birds, and shifting clouds of insects unclassified by the taxonomist, and deer, muskrat, fang-toothed cousins of the piranha, and creatures born to twitch in fear and die.

The chopper hovered. The pilot, a husky, weathered, gray-templed veteran, gave the team a badgering squint. "Welcome to a week in hell's furnace, you gyrenes. I'll go have a beer."

He had chosen and zeroed Point Exercise, a finger-shaped hummock about a mile in length. A relative clearing, grown in waist-high grass on its eastern end, beckoned as a landing pad.

The pilot carefully rechecked readings on the electronic dials before him and clicked a switch, programming the coordinates into the mini-computer for a return to this precise spot one week from today.

He brought the chopper down feather-light, and Gordon, Finklestein, and I spilled out—three men in fatigues hunched in the flicking shadow of the idling overhead rotor.

The pilot grinned and yelled a parting, "Have fun." And the helicopter was quickly up and away, leaving a small, empty moment.

"Home sweet home," Finklestein said, looking around. He was twenty years old, wiry and agile.

"Bring on the girls," Gordon added. A rawboned, slightly gawky, sandy-haired farm boy from Iowa, he listened to his words die in a muggy silence accented by the soft insect hum.

I'd spotted a probable campsite while the chopper had hovered, a shadowed glen about three hundred yards west of where we stood. "Let's see what the Everglades Hilton has to offer."

We strung out and walked, the grass slashing our calves. I was at point, senior in rank, age, experience—and size. I have not always been comfortable about my size. I stand six feet, seven inches, weigh in at two-forty. Gordon and Finklestein were by no means shorties, but I towered above them, and at the moment they seemed a bit grateful for my shadow.

A dozen yards, and the cloying heat swathed us in oily sweat. It was only a foretaste. Knives, matches, brains, and hands—tools for survival. Two concessions only had been made. In my hip pocket was the notebook in which I would keep a daily log—and which is now receiving this report. And Finklestein carried a portable short-wave transmitter, rigged with shoulder straps. It was insurance against the most desperate emergency.

Still, I thought of what we'd look like a week from today when we stepped aboard the helicopter. Baked out. Cheeks and noses peeling. Lumpy from insect bites. But I hadn't the slightest doubt we'd be wearing the cocksure grin of Marines at the end of maneuvers.

The glade looked even better than it had from the air. It was sheltered by twisted pines and cabbage palms, carpeted with a soft sponge of pine needles. Two stunted trees would anchor the southern corners of a tchiki, the open-sided shelter favored by the Seminoles of old.

By sunset, we were pioneering in style. Our campfire was a friendly flicker in a muggy twilight, our bodies were tired, and the details of a busy day ran together in our minds. Or at least in mine. We'd cut pole framing and fronds for the tchiki roof. Plaited cordage from slender vines. Split bamboo for fish spears and crab traps. Gordon had turned up a fifty-pound turtle and we had him staked out alive as larder of future fresh meat. Finklestein had trapped an enormous king snake. I'd robbed a quail's nest and climbed a cabbage palm to cut out the bud. Now we were belching pleasant echoes of a dinner of roast snake, baked eggs, and crisp, juicy palm fruit.

Under a bright moon we talked in the desultory way of men whose friendship needs little conversation. Gordon volunteered for first watch. I left him and Finklestein talking and sacked out under the tchiki. Another too-short bunk; the soles of my combat boots stuck out from the shadow of the thatch roof.

I lay there for a little while, liquidly tired, listening to sounds already ancient before man dressed out in his first skin. Skirlings . . . rustlings . . . basso frogs (frog legs for breakfast?) . . . snarlings . . . thrashings . . . screams, sometimes cut short . . .

I'm not sure just what awakened me. Maybe it was the impact of the club as it crushed Gordon's skull, or Finklestein's movements as he stirred from sleep during the final second of his life when the crude club rose and fell once more.

The first thing I consciously heard was an absolute silence. The writhing violence of the 'Glades had come to a total halt, and the silence, so sudden, was a ringing in my ears.

And while the silence deafened, the darkness became a gagging odor like something out of a slimy pit that had formed when the earth was young. It was the steam from the excretion of dinosaurs, the musk of a female creature long dead, the fetid effluvia of some unspeakable thing.

My first impression of the source of the smell was of two hairy, columnar legs standing beside the open-sided tchiki. As I reared up, spun, drew the trench knife, enormous hands grabbed the front roof and ripped it away.

I rolled through the open side, bounced to my feet away from the monstrous thing. I glimpsed Gordon and Finklestein sprawled in the open glade, their heads shattered. The thing had dropped its tree limb club to smash the tchiki and get to me. Its shadow engulfed me. I had an impression of a hairy black humanoid shape, about nine feet tall. Then I was enveloped by massive arms, and the smell of the thing shot down my throat, through my guts.

Maybe I screamed in a very un-Marinelike way. I'm not sure. I had the nightmarish certainty that I was going to be crushed and carried to some time-forgotten lair as dinner for a couple of hungry cubs.

The creature mewled, gibbered, and resisted my thrashings by crushing me against its sickening mass. I felt the tip of my knife bite into a yielding surface, and the thing barked in querulous anger and pain. For a second the embrace was uncertain, and I managed to break away.

I plunged through a thicket and ran. Heard my feet splash water and felt the slash of sawgrass. I looked over my shoulder at the shifting of shadows on the hummock, trying to separate the gigantic creature from the background blackness. It spotted me and called out, a bark-bark-barking note, high in pitch. The weird sound struck me as a pronouncement, a promise. I was the invader. I had hurt something that ruled here, and I must pay a price for that.

As I churned on through the sawgrass, my Marine training took hold of me again and my thoughts began to order themselves. Objective: survive the night; don't get lost; return to the campsite and the short-wave transmitter. Obstacle: I could hear the slashing of sawgrass as the thing narrowed the distance in long strides. I had no hope of outrunning it. And no chance if I faced it squarely, even as large and strong as I was by everyday measurements.

The shallow water thinned out and was gone. Moist black sand became firmer under my pounding feet. Dense jungle shadows closed about me. The next hummock was a couple of hundred yards south of the campsite.

I veered in that direction, ducked behind a giant banyan tree and stood sucking for breath. The night was silent for a moment. The thing, I knew, had reached the edge of the hummock, its night vision searching for me. It bark-barked a note of angry frustration, as if demanding that I stop this foolishness and give myself up to it.

I heard the thud of heavy footsteps and knew the banyan was poor cover. I broke away, going deeper into the hummock, burrowing through a dry thicket. Never mind the sounds, the dry rattlings that revealed the direction of my flight; I had matches in my hand now.

Scratch. Pouf. Wink of fire. I dropped one after another in the brush as I ran. If the first one didn't catch, I prayed the second or third would.

I burst out of the underbrush into a small clearing, changed directions, dropped belly flat, and wriggled into a maze of twisted pine trees. As I looked back, tongues of fire were lapping in the thicket. More than one of the matches had caught and touched off the dry grass.

There was a hesitant crackling, then a soft roar as more of the tinder-dry brush flamed. I saw the humanoid silhouette towering at the further edge of the thicket. It barked again, looking this way and that, still searching for me. Then it reeled back as the flames swept toward it.

I wormed down to the water's edge. This time, I didn't run. I stayed low, on all fours below the level of the sawgrass. Several yards out, I took my bearings. The Big Dipper, the North Star—I wanted to keep Polaris directly behind me and move due south. A subsequent trip due north, when I had the chance, would return me to the campsite and short-wave transmitter.

Half an hour later I crawled onto another hummock,

sprawling, taking painful breaths. Looking back, I could see the dark image of the monster towering above the sawgrass. Quarter of a mile behind me now. Slogging back and forth uncertainly, mewling and whining in the same angry frustration as before.

I lay, hands knotted, silently begging the creature to turn east, west, north—any direction but south. The fire had made it lose site of me and it seemed to be searching haphazardly. I was beginning to hope that the odds now were several dozen compass points in my favor.

Then I saw it come to a standstill. Its processes were working, crystallizing. As if with sudden decision, it began to move toward the hummock where I lay. I backed off, the sick emptiness working again in my belly. I wondered if the thing could smell me as I smelled it, and if my own odor was equally repulsive.

Always south . . . keeping the invisible, tenuous lifeline of direction between me and the transmitter. Every furlong, every hellish mile increased the risk of losing my fix on the campsite and transmitter forever. From a distance each hummock looked like all the others. How many hummocks? Ten thousand? If I did lose direction, the transmitter would become the proverbial needle in a haystack.

The night became a nightmare of fatigue, sawgrass and water, lattices of iron-hard mangrove in impenetrable tangles. Forever due south, Polaris winking behind me whenever I could see the sky.

Finally I collapsed under a great live oak, too exhausted to get up, too frightened to feel safe where I was. I lay there, my cheek against rotting humus that a week ago had been avid green vegetation, listening. Waiting for the echoes of giant footsteps.

But they didn't come, and I realized that my ears were trying to tell me something. Yes . . . once more the swamp shimmered with its normal predawn sounds; it no longer crouched in silence because the thing was there. The creature must have lost my trail . . .

My spry old grandmother was at my bedside, her face filled with concern in its soft cloud of fine gray hair. I was ten years old and my temperature had been a hundred and three, and my grandmother was smiling and touching my forehead with a cool cloth. "Hi there, Mr. James C. Kelly! I do declare, the delirious boy who had a franzy is back with us, the nasty old fever all gone. What are we having for breakfast, Jimmy the Rugged?" . . .

Then my senses struggled up out of the dream, and there was merciless sun-glare, dappled through gnarled pines and shaggy wild palms. There was timeless emptiness and the hiss of insects. I wasn't ten; and the "franzy" had been for real. A hint of the creature's smell from the moment of close contact still clung to me, nauseatingly.

I sat up, took hold of a knotty sapling, and pulled to my feet. The sun was still low in the east, but the morning was already a shroud of heat.

Working against muscle stiffness, I walked across the narrow island, keeping the sun on my right. I looked north—and a small, bright jolt went through me. I was anything but lost. In the distance a thin feather of pale gray smoke high in the sky marked the location of the hummock I had set on fire. I had picked up a spin-off dividend. The masses of green stuff on the hummock would smolder and smoke for perhaps days—a beacon two hundred yards south of Point E, the campsite.

I wanted food, a bath. My own stink was overlaid by the creature's effluvium. My belly rumbled emptily. I imagined dining on roast portions from Gordon's fifty-pound turtle tethered at the campsite while I transmitted an endless Mayday on the radio. But the thought was a crutch; it didn't ease my heavy sorrow. I was alive, on a day that Gordon and Finklestein would not see. They would be my first objective at Point E.

I laid the mutilated bodies side by side, expressed a prayer over them, and, burial being out of the question, covered them with a makeshift shield of palm fronds. Then I crossed the clearing to where the radio was—

A tearing sensation went through me. And I squatted slowly and fingered the wreckage of the short-wave transmitter. A heavy foot had come down on it in passing, crushing it under what must have been at least five hundred pounds of weight.

I could only hunker there, suspended in the prehistoric immensity of this place. I felt eyes watching me, felt the swamp humming a baleful promise all around me. Bamboo clicking softly, like the rattle of clods on my coffin.

Drawing a breath, I fought down the spooky feeling. "The hell with you!" I muttered at the swamp, and pushed to my feet. I wasn't dead yet. This was still a Survival Exercise.

My first task was to kill and roast the turtle—rations for a trip north. Somewhere in that direction lay the only mark of civilization I had a hope of reaching, the old Tamiami Trail which crosses the 'Glades from Naples on the Gulf to Miami on the Atlantic.

By midday I figured I'd made five or six miles. My surroundings didn't show it. From any vantage point the 'Glades were the same, an expanding universe of sawgrass and water dotted with hummocks like minor galaxies without number.

In the late afternoon I finally stopped to rest. I stripped off and bathed in a waist-deep lagoon off the perimeter of a hummock. Scrubbed myself with sand. But some of the smell of the monster lingered, whether in my pores or in my imagination. I no longer knew which.

I thought of a legend an old Seminole had once told me. It was the story of Stuestaw Enawchee. Literally translated, the words come out to mean "too much body." In the old legendary application, the Stuestaw Enawchee were the gigantic beings from some netherworld that had inhabited the Rivers of Grass since the time of creation. They had come out of the great swamp to war on the first Seminoles a thousand generations before the white man appeared. The People, so went the legend, had a shaman who was sent down from heaven with a magic herb with which he anointed his body as he went into the swamp to confront the creatures. The herb killed off so many of the Stuestaw Enawchee that they began to fear the People and retreated into the great swamp, and the People were able to live in peace.

Trekking on northward, I thought about the Stuestaw Enawchee. From what I had seen I was certain that this legend was, like many others, grounded in fact. Troy and Ur were legends until archeologists went after them with their picks and shovels. The African legends of a man-thing were legends no more after Leakey turned up his first fossilized find. In the present case, Captain McCabe, it is imperative that you not dismiss the Stuestaw Enawchee—the SE—as a figment of a Marine's heat-blasted mind. At the dawn of man, there must have been many such descendants of something that came crawling out of primordial slime, isolated and indigenous to this tropical wilderness a mapmaker would ultimately label the Everglades. The aboriginal ancestors of the Seminoles had discovered a poison, a magic herb, a bait that would kill off the SEs, beat them back, until it *seemed* that the hideous beings had vanished forever.

But forever is a long, long time . . .

As the gray fur of twilight spread over the reaches, I slogged onto a hummock and was content to sprawl belly flat for a while. I guessed that I'd covered about fifteen miles. Not much of a hike for a six-foot-seven-inch Marine? Sir, I hope you never have to try it through sawgrass.

I half-dozed, not letting myself think of where I was. After a little, I roused myself, ate a piece of roast turtle, and then curled in for the night in a tiny alcove inside a clump of wild palms. It was not much of a bivouac, but I slept anyway.

And then, when the night was old and strained in a hush, a mist came seeping out of a cauldron from a time when dinosaurs were dying . . . a body dew . . . a musk . . . a nauseating essence coiling over my flesh . . .

My eyes snapped open. I admit to choking back a scream. My heart felt as if it would burst through my chest. The palms rustled as the SE parted the fronds. The slow steps thudded, heavy beats measuring off the remnants of my life. The great hairy head blocked off the light of a dying moon.

I twisted around and got out through a break between

the palms. Into the water once more. Running, fighting aside the sawgrass.

Behind me the SE barked churlishly.

I floundered onto a hummock. Wrong direction, headed south away from the old trail. But I had no choice. The thing was herding me back toward the depths of the 'Glades.

I could hear the splashing of the huge feet. Nocturnal creatures . . . quiescent by day, but by night imbued with powers of which I had no knowledge. I felt the sick certainty that the thing had antennae, a sense unknown to human beings—a guidance system like the sonar of a bat, the instinct of a Capistrano swallow, the built-in controls of an SAM missile. A tool evolved a thousand millennia ago to compensate for the bulk that made it hard for an SE to slip up undetected on its prey. No need to crouch and spring when the creature could dog its quarry to exhaustion.

Why had I been given a day's reprieve? Because the SE's unique function was impaired by solar radiation, the way sunspots interfere with our own sub-light-level transmissions? Because the thing saw better at night in the infrared range? It didn't matter now; I was already scrambling onto another hummock, hearing the creature coming through sawgrass and underbrush, forcing me southward.

I turned right and went off the end of the hummock. Calmer now. Again staying low, taking the cover of the sawgrass.

I eeled my way across to the next island as dawn came, hot and angry red out of the east. Tearing through a wall of vines, I squished up onto firmer ground. A clearing spread before me. My footsteps wavered. In the middle of the glen was a low mound about ten feet long. And in the gray light I realized it was not a natural mound at all. I jarred to a halt, staring. The SE lay before me, stretched on its back as if asleep. How had it circled and got here? Why didn't it move?

By then I had the knife in my hand. Then the scent came, that permeating muskiness, seeping through the dawn . . . from *behind* me. I heard crashings in the underbrush in the direction from which I'd come.

In a crouch I circled the clearing, eased into the shallow water, took cover in the sawgrass. So there were two of them. A living SE with the single thought of pursuit in its primeval brain. And one dead thing in the clearing. Not like any animal, either of them. Nor like any human. A gigantic blending of the two.

Looking back through the spiny green, I saw the living SE arrive at the side of the dead one. The living one stopped, and for a brief moment I seemed to be forgotten as it knelt beside the dead creature, took one of the enormous dead hands and pressed it to a broad, hairy cheek. The living one's head lifted and the shrill bark-bark became a lament of pain and heartbreak.

I understood, then. The living SE was a female, and her mate had fallen ill and died.

I was held by the depths of the SE's—Essie's—grief as she hunkered beside her mate. I wondered if this had been part of her purpose, to bring me here for a sharing of her bereavement and suffering. If so, it was a ritual beyond my comprehension.

I faded back quietly, working my way through the sawgrass and canebreaks as the sun rose higher. I knew when she returned to my trail. Through the brightening heat came her high-pitched mewling, the note of loneliness and despair that had so often told me her position. The cries became less strident as the sun neared its zenith. Finally, there was only the insect hum and the sound of my own exhausted breathing.

At midday I looked out through a screen of brush on the island where I'd finally come to roost. I saw no sign of Essie, but I knew she was out there, waiting for nightfall again.

I took a bearing. Far to the southeast a thin sliver of smoke hung in the brazen sky, marking the approximate location of Point E. If I survived, I would meet the helicopter there as scheduled. If not, I would leave this report beside the bodies of my two comrades.

Meanwhile, my body machinery demanded attention. I dug out some coontie root with the knife and munched the starchy provender of the old-time Seminoles. It was flat, taste-less, but filling and nourishing. Then I rolled into the water, clothed, to cool off. A mess of a Marine, face hamburgered from insect bites, each hair a painful quill in the tenderness of my sun-burned scalp . . .

Afterward I crawled into the palmetto shadows and slept.

Now, Captain McCabe, I have regained enough strength to move out again. My destination is Point E, and I would like to com-plete this report insofar as possible in case I am not there to file a verbal report when the helicopter returns for the pickup of the survival team.

If I'm missing, when you view the bodies of good men

such as Gordon and Finklestein you must give all due thought to my explanation. There are things unknown in the recesses of the 'Glades, Captain McCabe. You must accept that.

Just as I am accepting the clarity of certain factors.

I know why Essie didn't club me to death in the first attack on the campsite. She had seen that I was the biggest of the three strange SE-oid creatures that had invaded her domain. She had a reason to spare the largest.

I know the meaning of her mewlings and whimperings, her high-pitched baring notes of entreaty.

I can begin to understand, to imagine, how the big, dead male must have felt when he in vigorous life smelled that primeval odor, the exudation of musk, that perfume of hers. Now he is dead, and the laws of her nature can't be set aside, any more than we could stop a female deer from exuding her mating scent when she is in heat.

Essie is a passion-heavy female in full season, on the prowl for a mate.

I can't help feeling for her innocence, her helplessness in her hormonal situation. But even though I feel compassion for her, I have my knife out and ready. If I am denied sanctuary at Point E, one of us will die.

She is out there now in the lengthening shadows, mewling and whimpering and bark-barking her impatience. She is out there, sir, singing her hellish song of love . . .

SWAMP HORROR

Will Smith and R. J. Robbins

Mayhap it was the influence of the moon's rays playing on my recumbent form—or was it a subtle stealing of that eerie sound into the innermost recesses of my subconscious mind? I had suddenly awakened from a profound slumber, every nerve atingle with the premonition of evil. It was as if a ghostly touch on my brow had called me from the enshrouding incubus of sleep and brought me up all standing with fright! The whole atmosphere seemed surcharged with an electric something that still lingers in my memory. Cursing myself for a timid fool, I crossed to the window, through which the moonlight streamed in sickly fashion. And now, as I gazed out upon the vista of grey field and ink-black wood I became conscious of a strange stillness, a complete silencing of all the familiar sounds of nature, becoming with each moment more oppressive. Hark! What was that? Reverberating over the distances, horribly loud, came a frenzied, screeching cry!

As I stood at the open window, wildly straining my ears, it came again. This time the cry had almost a human quality, but there had also crept into it a suggestion of eeriness that made my flesh tingle all over, and a tremor ran over my spine.

Now, I am not a coward, and since early childhood I have never feared the dark nor anything which might lurk under its cover. Still, to an essentially city-bred man such an occurrence as this was bound to have a fear-inspiring flavour. I had always, indeed, detested anything rural, even before I suffered the frightful experience I am about to relate; had always entertained for the woods and swamps a nameless, unreasoning fear. It was in response to that same fear that I had migrated from the ancestral residence at the tender age of sixteen, getting a job as errand-boy in the near-by city. After this I had held down several minor jobs until I had finally found my métier in telegraphy. It was the latter occupation that was earning me my living when the awful horror of the swamp took place.

That morning Sam Falton, operator and general factotum at my home-town station, had started the ball rolling by engaging me in some small-talk on the wire. Both being desirous of learning the Phillips press code, we had, for practice, been couching every possible word of our conversation in that language. Apparently he had decided to sign off for the time being when he gave a signal for me to hold the wire a moment. His next words gave me a severe jolt.

Literally, they were, "ML MAN JS CA IN SES U BTR CM SES TRS SMG MYX AB IT UR DAD BN MSG NRY A WK." These words, unintelligible to the reader, were sufficient to cause me to demand leave of absence for an indefinite period. Translated, they are: "Mail man just came in. Says you better come. Says there's something mysterious about it; your dad been missing nearly a week!"

I had about decided to go back to bed when I heard the sound repeated again and again. It was nearer this time, and sounded like the wail of some creature in a frenzy of torture. At times it would end in a long-drawn-out, strangling, rattling howl that made my blood run cold.

Could this have anything to do with my father's disappearance? The sounds might have been made by madman or beast, or by something altogether unearthly. My mind, ever used to quick decisions, was instantly made up. I resolved to see.

The night was hot and humid, and in the hollows a heavy ground-fog was beginning to manifest itself, and I suspected that before sun-up the air would be pretty chilly. Plainly, time was short, so I contented myself with a pair of trousers, a sleeveless jersey, and a pair of tennis-shoes which lay at hand. Snatching a hastily lighted lantern, I dashed out into the pulsing night.

The sounds had evidently issued from a stretch of forest about a quarter-mile to the rear of the house, and towards this I made my way. The ground-fog had by this time become quite thick, so that at times I had to grope my way through it. Nature had resumed all her various discordant notes. As I entered the forest the odour of decayed vegetation and mould smote my nostrils. The lantern, a relic of bygone days, cast a feeble circle of light which but served to intensify the surrounding gloom. My thoughts, as I struggled through the underbrush and thickets, were anything but cheerful.

At times fantastically formed roots took on the appearance of serpents ever waiting to drag me down. That I did not fall on more than one occasion was more a result of good luck than of agility on my part. I must have proceeded into the depths of the woods for at least a mile when suddenly the fearful cry came again, now in a direction more to my left and somewhat nearer. I shivered and grasped the lantern more tightly, meantime cursing the folly that had sent me on this wild quest unarmed. Then again the cry—fearsomely close!

At this juncture, grown careless of the terrain beneath my feet, I suddenly stumbled violently over a rotting log lying directly in my path. I remember taking a desperate grip on the lantern, which barely prevented it from flying from my hand, when—a most unearthly scream resounded in the bushes not ten feet away, and a huge body dashed against me, brushing me flat and extinguishing the lantern. Before it died the flame flared up into momentary brilliancy, giving me a passing glimpse of a great, wolf-like creature with blood-slavering jaws and terrible glistening fangs!

I struck my head as I fell, and my senses reeled.

I have no distinct recollection of my return to the house, I must have lain unconscious in the forest for some time, for it was nearly dawn when I finally got up and somehow made my way out. Once in bed, I dropped again into oblivion, and did not awake until some hours later.

Since my father had had no hired man, and mother had died long years before, there was no one to call me or prepare the meals. When I finally found the ambition to rise and dress, my first act was to get together a meal, for I intended to cover a lot of ground during the day, and felt that my stomach should be well fortified. Had I known what lay ahead of me I doubt if I could have eaten anything!

I had about finished my bacon and coffee when I was aroused from a momentary abstraction by a sound from the outside. A quick glance around the premises revealing nothing, I was about to give up the search, when I heard it again; but this time it was a low moan, and of a character which I recognized. Hurrying to the back shed, I threw open the door. There, brilliantly limned in the shaft of sunlight that streamed in, lay the still form of a huge wolf-hound!

I started back aghast. Could this gaunt creature be our good old Fang, the pet with whom father and I had used to spend so many happy hours, and who had greeted me with such rough joy only yesterday? Yes, it was indeed he, for at my call the faithful fellow struggled feebly to his feet, and, swaying drunkenly, wagged a heroic tail.

But to what a terrible state the animal had been reduced! His whole form was wasted to a painful thinness. The skin, hairless in patches, was nearly white, colourless. The poor creature seemed to be suffering from what I could attribute to no other cause than such a weakness as is caused by a heavy loss of blood. And yet, minutely examining every inch of the slackened skin, I could find not a scratch, *no visible wound whatever!*

I lost no time in feeding the dog, and did my poor best at doctoring him. My efforts, aided no doubt by the vitality of his ancient wild ancestry, were sufficiently successful to enable the animal after a while to recover enough strength to walk without difficulty, and even to run and fetch sticks. But I knew well that it would be many days before he could regain the robust sturdiness of the day before.

What, I kept wondering, could have been the agency that had brought Fang to this pitiful condition? What could have drained his veins so completely without leaving a single mark? Where had he been the night before, and what frightful thing could have reduced him to the state of abject fear that caused him to dash so madly through the forest uttering those agonized, strangled screams? For I was convinced that the creature I had encountered last night under such terrifying circumstances was none other than Fang, his really monstrous size enlarged in my terror-stricken eyes to gigantic proportions.

But I could swear to the blood I had seen dripping from the beast's jaws. Whence had that come?

The horrible answer to all these questions was vouchsafed me that very day.

It being by now early afternoon, I realized that if I were to search for my father today I should have to start at once. As I locked up the house preparatory to setting out I tried to recall to mind the general topography of the region.

The farm, which has been in the possession of our family more than a century, is of considerable extent, and is made up mostly of timberland and swamp, there being only a few acres of open land. Directly to the rear of the house is a large forest tract, some parts of which have not been penetrated by men for years. Beyond this is an almost unexplored waste known as Marvin's Swamp.

Legend has it that Old Man Marvin, who owned the farm

before it came into my family, died in this vicinity under mysterious circumstances, and it is thought that his bones found their last resting-place at the bottom of the morass. The only clue to his fate was furnished by his ancient shotgun and a few blood-stains found near a stagnant pool in the depths of the marsh. I shudder as I recall the terrible solution I myself was enabled to furnish to this mystery of long ago!

In starting on the search my footsteps followed almost without deviation the course I had pursued the previous night, but this time I was not alone. The great wolf-hound was now my guide, and I soon discovered he was following a scent. Indeed, I had considerable difficulty at times in keeping up with him, so great was his evident desire to lead me to a definite spot.

This forest tract is in itself extensive, and is pretty wild. My father had never allowed anyone to hunt here except members of the family, and as a result the place abounded with partridges, squirrels, rabbits, and other small game. Occasionally, even, I would get a glimpse of a deer or a fox as it leapt away at my approach. Everywhere was the odour of pine, hemlock, and decaying vegetation. The silence of the place was so profound that the smallest sound was immediately noticeable, and even the snapping of twigs underfoot and the breaking of dead branches as I made my way through the thickets served to keep my nerves continually on edge. At length we had penetrated to the other side of the forest, and I found myself at the edge of Marvin's Swamp. Somehow, call it premonition or what you will, a cold shiver passed up my spine as I gazed upon this dreary stretch, and I glanced around apprehensively.

Nothing appeared within my field of vision which could

possibly be alarming, so after a brief hesitation I followed the big wolf-hound on the trail. Within a few minutes I could see that we were heading towards the vilest part of the great morass, and again that strange presentiment of evil came over me. The ground was getting softer now, and small sinkholes became more and more numerous. For an hour we pushed on, the way becoming more difficult every minute. The vegetation grew here very rankly, and had become almost entirely aquatic. Cat-o'-nine-tails were now in evidence everywhere, especially about the spot where the dog now impatiently awaited me. This spot was at what marked the centre of Marvin's Swamp—a small stream of almost stagnant water known as Dead River.

The name is rather a dignity, for Dead River is in reality little more than an arm of the main pool of the swamp. Its course had once been traced back and found to extend through the worst part of the region for about a mile and thence into the hills, where its only source was found to be a series of small springs. At the bank of this repulsive waterway I stopped and began to examine the locality closely. Finally I found what I had been looking for, namely a multitude of foot-prints in the soft mud. A glance at these was enough to convince me as to who had made the tracks, but such evidence was nothing to that which now met my eye. For a little to the right of the trail, half hidden in a tuft of rank grass into which it had evidently been unwittingly dropped, lay Father's familiar old hunting-knife! I bowed my head; all hope had left me.

But I had little time to stand here sadly musing, for the strange behaviour of the dog now claimed my attention. He stood a little way ahead of me along the bank, trembling from head to drooping tail; first whining beseechingly back at me, then snarling with a sort of frightened ferocity as he gazed ahead to where the trail led into a dark, evil-looking glade. Absently dropping the knife into a trousers pocket, I hastened to follow his fear-halted lead; and my quest came to an abrupt end!

The glade—what a hideous spot it was! The river at this point was but a desolation of cat-o'-nine-tails, rank growths, and green, slimy water. Little green lizards basked dreamily on rotting logs and swam lazily about in the stagnant pool. Brilliant-coloured dragon-flies poised for a breathless instant over foul, exotic lilies, only to dart away into black, hot aisles of the swamp. Leeches were everywhere, and now and again a water-snake came zig-zagging among the lily-pads in search of prey. More noisome still, the bottom of the pool and its filthy banks were littered with all kinds of dead creatures—all sizes of bodies, from those of tiny squirrels up to the carcasses of bob-cats and even deer. Not one of them bore a visible wound, and every one was almost colourless. Those soaking in the murky water were bloated into gross exaggerations of their proper sizes, but those on the banks were dry, shriveled, shrunken things! All this I noted as in a wondering dream, the while I gazed on the body of my father.

It lay on the bank with one leg dangling in the water, the limbs weirdly contorted, as though the man had succumbed only after a terrific struggle. Nearly demoralized, I flew frantically at the body, seizing it by the shoulders and yanking it clear of the horrible pool. A hasty examination sufficed to show that Father had met the same mysterious fate that had taken toll of so many lives in this hateful place.

I had barely made the discovery when I was completely undone by a distant, long-drawn-out howl—the frightened bay of the wolf-hound. His mission accomplished, he had promptly deserted, leaving me alone with my dead.

I was not long to wonder why!

What was the terrible fate that could strike down a man in the sanguine glow of physical strength and activity and leave this shriveled, white, bloodless death? And that, too, without leaving a single mark on the husk of a body! To be sure, the clothing was covered with dried blood-stains, but whence had the blood come? Was there not some tiny wound which I in my first frantic pawing of the corpse had overlooked—perhaps the two little purple holes which I shudderingly remembered were supposed to be the mark of venomous snake-bites? I stooped again, and, clenching my jaws to still my chattering teeth, began a careful search of the drained thing that had been my father. And as the fruitless quest went on there came again that hush, that awed stilling of the myriad sounds of this rank nature about me.

I became conscious of each noise, as it were, when it had ceased to beat its note on my ears. The shrilling of the frogs first dropped out of nature's discordant symphony, to be followed by the chirp of the crickets, the various low bird-twitterings and rustlings, and other sounds, most of them to me fearsomely unidentified. Now all that remained was the droning of bees, punctuated at longish intervals by the mournful *sol do-do-do-do-lo do-o-o* of a far-away swamp robin.

Now, after one dismally long-drawn-out call, the bird became silent, and the only sound left in the steamy, fetid swamp world was that bee-hum. This now seemed slowly to increase in volume until finally the very air became charged and volatile with its menace. At last I could endure the deafening sound no longer, and, ear-drums bursting with the throbbing, zooming waves—smothered in them, overwhelmed, I toppled over in a black faint.

I was destined soon to bless that fainting-fall, for I was to realize it had saved me from a fate worthy of the ingenuity of a thousand fiends—the same ravaged death that had claimed my father.

Of course, I could not have lain unconscious more than a minute or two, but at the time it seemed ages before I opened my eyes— opened them to a sun-drenched, somehow less fearful world—to find myself sprawled on my back, evidently in a little depression. Of this hollow, the bottom seemed covered with some wet, sticky substance, which to my not over-critical bones made a rather pleasant couch.

Nature had resumed her normal note, and I became gratefully conscious that the horrible droning of bees was no longer in evidence. As I again closed my eyes in response to a certain feeling of lassitude that bound me I wondered if it had been a sound from the outside world or if it had come from within me. Dreamily revolving the affair in my mind, I was inclined to believe the whole thing—the hush, the drumming in my ears, and the fainting—had been caused by the gradual weakening of my faculties. But then how to account for that weakening?

The mystery was getting too deep for me, and I almost decided to give it all up and flee from this hellish swamp, sending someone in after Father's body. At any rate, I could not lie long dreaming in this soft bed. Lazily I opened my eyes; wearily I stretched out an arm; limply I let it fall at my side; and then, screeching with all my poor strength, I leapt to my feet. My outflung arm had dropped with a syrupy splash in what was revealed to my popping eyes as thickening, dark-red blood!

And now began the horror—ugh! an experience so incredibly, grotesquely horrid that recollection of its lewd details now halts my pen and imbues me with stark nausea. If I had disliked and distrusted the woods and waste places before, my feeling was nothing compared to the seething, loathing hate that grips me now at the mention of that dread word "swamp."

Reeling giddily, my unmanning utterly completed by the sickening realization that I had been lolling so softly in a bed of blood, I had time only to clutch at a low-hanging vine for support before the things—oh, those fat, slime-sweating, crawling *things*—came on! There seemed to be hundreds of them—snail-shaped things as large as dogs—hemming me in on every side. With a slow, irresistible purpose they advanced in a horrible silence. As they closed in, their silence became broken by a nasty greasy sound as of molasses being lazily lifted and stirred with a million sticks. Now they were upon me, and I ran amuck!

I leapt on the nearest and tried to scuff them into the earth; I beat them foolishly with my fists; I sought to hug them off my heaving chest; I rolled over and over them; I tore at their filthy bodies with my teeth; the while I uttered one tortured shriek after another. But in my unarmed state I was no match for the horde, and the things continued in their deadly purpose, bearing me down and beginning to fasten themselves on to every part of me. At last my frenzied yells were stilled by a clammy body laid across the whole lower half of my face; and now my eyes, rolling in dumb agony, encountered the foulest scene of all, and I understood.

The blood-filled hollow in which I had been lying! Crowding around all sides of it like pigs at a trough were a dozen of the monsters, greedily and with many blubbery swilling sounds absorbing the clotting gore!

Now I knew the fate that had befallen Father, had taken old Marvin years before, had claimed the deer and other animals, had dragged at Fang when he had searched out Father's body, and now bade fair to add me to those other letted *cadavers*. Yes, I could see it all now, could understand anything in this rank world of evil growths.

Bloodsuckers! That's what they were! Great, fat, overgrown leeches; spawned of the filth and grown here to this morbid size by centuries of breeding and interbreeding in the lushness. Oh, the horror that swept me!

It was when the obscene feast drew to a close that I thanked God for the fall I had taken a few minutes before when I had fainted, for there was now revealed in the bottom of the depression the empty, sack-like body of one of the gigantic leeches. Evidently the scout of the main herd, it had stolen and fastened itself to my back as I stooped over the remains of my father. Its slow sapping of my life's blood had caused the humming in my ears and finally the deathly faint which had saved my life and been the thing's undoing. For in falling I had landed on my back on a jagged bit of stone, which had pierced and emptied the creature, filling my resting-place with blood.

The sharp tip of the rock now protruded through the flattened carcass and became my inspiration. What did it suggest to me? I was fast sinking into a soft, black oblivion and could not think—did not care to, particularly. Now another slimy body drew along my head and settled itself in such a way as to cover my eyes, shutting out the scene completely. Still the memory of that rock sliver persisted and disturbed me vaguely. What did it remind me of, anyway? Well, I didn't know—never mind. But, yes, I *did* know! Now I had it—a knife! Father's knife, in my pocket!

Gone in a breath was that deathly languor. I became imbued with the strength of desperation. I heaved, I threshed—one hand came clear. Lifting the arm, almost unmindful of the weight of a monster still clinging to it, I worked my hand between two foul bodies into my pocket. And now I drew it out, clutching that blessed knife!

Butchery! Blood!

My first kill was the bloated thing that lay across my scalp and eyes. But what a flood of gore now cascaded over me, filling hair, ears, and eyes! Blinking an eye, I plunged the knife into the stinking monster that blocked my mouth—and was again soaked in a green-streaked red deluge. My mouth free, I found strength once more to yell, but now a note of battle and triumph in the cry!

Slashing and hacking, I gained my feet. Now I seemed to swim in a sea of blood as, sinking the knife to the hilt again and again, I finally freed my legs. And even as I had used my mouth the instant I had cleared it, so now I used my legs. Stumbling, groping, crying, laughing, I ran.

PLAINS

THE VALLEY OF THE SPIDERS

H. G. Wells

Towards midday the three pursuers came abruptly round a bend in the torrent bed upon the sight of a very broad and spacious valley. The difficult and winding trench of pebbles along which they had tracked the fugitives for so long expanded to a broad slope, and with a common impulse the three men left the trail, and rode to a low eminence set with olive-dun trees, and there halted, the two others as became them, a little behind the man with the silver-studded bridle.

For a space they scanned the great expanse below them with eager eyes. It spread remoter and remoter, with only a few clusters of sere thorn bushes here and there, and the dim suggestions of some now waterless ravine to break its desolation of yellow grass. Its purple distances melted at last into the bluish slopes of the further hills—hills it might be of a greener kind—

and above them invisibly supported, and seeming indeed to hang in the blue, were the snow-clad summits of mountains—that grew larger and bolder to the north-westward as the sides of the valley drew together. And westward the valley opened until a distant darkness under the sky told where the forests began. But the three men looked neither east nor west, but only steadfastly across the valley.

The gaunt man with the scarred lip was the first to speak. "Nowhere," he said, with a sigh of disappointment in his voice. "But after all, they had a full day's start."

"They don't know we are after them," said the little man on the white horse.

"*She* would know," said the leader bitterly, as if speaking to himself.

"Even then they can't go fast. They've got no beast but the mule, and all today the girl's foot has been bleeding—"

The man with the silver bridle flashed a quick intensity of rage on him. "Do you think I haven't seen that?" he snarled.

"It helps, anyhow," whispered the little man to himself.

The gaunt man with the scarred lip stared impassively.

"They can't be over the valley," he said. "If we ride hard—"

He glanced at the white horse and paused.

"Curse all white horses!" said the man with the silver bridle and turned to scan the beast his curse included.

The little man looked down between the melancholy ears of his steed.

"I did my best," he said.

The two others stared again across the valley for a space. The gaunt man passed the back of his hand across the scarred lip.

"Come up!" said the man who owned the silver bridle, suddenly. The little man started and jerked his rein, and the horse hooves of the three made a multitudinous faint pattering upon the withered grass as they turned back towards the trail. . .

They rode cautiously down the long slope before them, and so came through a waste of prickly twisted bushes and strange dry shapes of horny branches that grew amongst the rocks, into the level below. And there the trail grew faint, for the soil was scanty, and the only herbage was this scorched dead straw that lay upon the ground. Still, by hard scanning, by leaning beside the horse's neck and pausing ever and again, even these white men could contrive to follow after their prey.

There were trodden places, bent and broken blades of the coarse grass, and ever and again the sufficient intimation of a footmark. And once the leader saw a brown smear of blood where the half-caste girl may have trod. And at that under his breath he cursed her for a fool.

The gaunt man checked his leader's tracking, and the little man on the white horse rode behind, a man lost in a dream. They rode one after another, the man with the silver bridle led the way, and they spoke never a word. After a time it came to the little man on the white horse that the world was very still. He started out of his dream. Besides the minute noises of their horses and equipment, the whole great valley kept the brooding quiet of a painted scene.

Before him went his master and his fellow, each intently leaning forward to the left, each impassively moving with the paces of his horse; their shadows went before them—still, noiseless, tapering attendants; and nearer a crouched cool shape was his own. He looked about him. What was it had gone? Then he remembered the reverberation from the banks of the gorge and the perpetual accompaniment of shifting, jostling pebbles. And, moreover—? There was no breeze. That was it! What a vast, still place it was, a monotonous afternoon slumber. And the sky open and blank, except for a somber veil of haze that had gathered in the upper valley.

He straightened his back, fretted with his bridle, puckered his lips to whistle, and simply sighed. He turned in his saddle for a time, and stared at the throat of the mountain gorge out of which they had come. Blank! Blank slopes on either side, with never a sign of a decent beast or tree—much less a man. What a land it was! What a wilderness! He dropped again into his former pose.

It filled him with a momentary pleasure to see a wry stick of purple black flash out into the form of a snake, and vanish amidst the brown. After all, the infernal valley was alive. And then, to rejoice him still more, came a breath across his face, a whisper that came and went, the faintest inclination of a stiff black-antlered bush upon a crest, the first intimations of a possible breeze. Idly he wetted his finger, and held it up.

He pulled up sharply to avoid a collision with the gaunt man, who had stopped at fault upon the trail. Just at that guilty moment he caught his master's eye looking towards him.

For a time he forced an interest in the tracking. Then, as they rode on again, he studied his master's shadow and hat and shoulder appearing and disappearing behind the gaunt man's nearer contours. They had ridden four days out of the very limits of the world into this desolate place, short of water, with nothing but a strip of dried meat under their saddles, over rocks and mountains, where surely none but these fugitives had ever been before—for *that!*

And all this was for a girl, a mere willful child! And the man had whole cityfuls of people to do his basest bidding—girls, women! Why in the name of passionate folly *this* one in particular? asked the little man, and scowled at the world, and licked his parched lips with a blackened tongue. It was the way of the master, and that was all he knew. Just because she sought to evade him. . . .

His eye caught a whole row of high-plumed canes bending in unison, and then the tails of silk that hung before his neck flapped and fell. The breeze was growing stronger. Somehow it took the stiff stillness out of things—and that was well.

"Hullo!" said the gaunt man.

All three stopped abruptly.

"What?" asked the master. "What?"

"Over there," said the gaunt man, pointing up the valley. "What?"

"Something coming towards us."

And as he spoke a yellow animal crested a rise and came bearing down upon them. It was a big wild dog, coming before the wind, tongue out, at a steady pace, and running with such an intensity of purpose that he did not seem to see the horsemen he approached. He ran with his nose up, following, it was plain, neither scent nor quarry. As he drew nearer the little man felt for his sword. "He's mad," said the gaunt rider.

"Shout!" said the little man and shouted.

The dog came on. Then when the little man's blade was

already out, it swerved aside and went panting by them and past. The eyes of the little man followed its flight. "There was no foam," he said. For a space the man with the silver-studded bridle stared up the valley. "Oh, come on!" he cried at last. "What does it matter?" and jerked his horse into movement again.

The little man left the insoluble mystery of a dog that fled from nothing but the wind, and lapsed into profound musings on human character. "Come on!" he whispered to himself. "Why should it be given to one man to say 'Come on!' with that stupendous violence of effect. Always, all his life, the man with the silver bridle has been saying that. If *I* said it—!" thought the little man. But people marvelled when the master was disobeyed even in the wildest things. This half-caste girl seemed to him, seemed to everyone, mad—blasphemous almost. The little man, by way of comparison, reflected on the gaunt rider with the scarred lip, as stalwart as his master, as brave and, indeed, perhaps braver, and yet for him there was obedience, nothing but to give obedience duly and stoutly. . . .

Certain sensations of the hands and knees called the little man back to more immediate things. He became aware of something. He rode up beside his gaunt fellow. "Do you notice the horses?" he said in an undertone.

The gaunt face looked interrogation.

"They don't like this wind," said the little man, and dropped behind as the man with the silver bridle turned upon him.

"It's all right," said the gaunt-faced man.

They rode on again for a space in silence. The foremost two rode downcast upon the trail, the hindmost man watched the haze that crept down the vastness of the valley, nearer and nearer, and noted how the wind grew in strength moment by moment. Far away on the left he saw a line of dark bulks—wild hog perhaps, galloping down the valley, but of that he said nothing, nor did he remark again upon the uneasiness of the horses.

And then he saw first one and then a second great white ball, a great shining white ball like a gigantic head of thistledown, that drove before the wind athwart the path. These balls soared high in the air, and dropped and rose again and caught for a moment, and hurried on and passed, but at the sight of them the restlessness of the horses increased.

Then presently he saw that more of these drifting globes —and then soon very many more—were hurrying towards him down the valley.

They became aware of a squealing. Athwart the path a huge boar rushed, turning his head but for one instant to glance at them, and then hurtling on down the valley again. And at that, all three stopped and sat in their saddles, staring into the thickening haze that was coming upon them.

"If it were not for this thistledown—" began the leader.

But now a big globe came drifting past within a score of yards of them. It was really not an even sphere at all, but a vast, soft, ragged, filmy thing, a sheet gathered by the corners, an aerial jelly fish, as it were, but rolling over and over as it advanced, and trailing long, cobwebby threads and streamers that floated in its wake.

"It isn't thistledown," said the little man.

"I don't like the stuff," said the gaunt man.

And they looked at one another.

"Curse it!" cried the leader. "The air's full of it up there. If it keeps on at this pace long, it will stop us altogether.

An instinctive feeling, such as lines out a herd of deer at the approach of some ambiguous thing, prompted them to turn their horses to the wind, ride forwards for a few paces, and stare at that advancing multitude of floating masses. They came on before the wind with a sort of smooth swiftness, rising and falling noiselessly, sinking to the earth, rebounding high, soaring—all with a perfect unanimity, with a still, deliberate assurance.

Right and left of the horsemen the pioneers of this strange army passed. At one that rolled along the ground, breaking shapelessly and trailing out reluctantly into long grappling ribbons and bands, all three horses began to shy and dance. The master was seized with a sudden, unreasonable impatience. He cursed the drifted globes roundly. "Get on!" he cried; "get on! What do these things matter? How can they matter? Back to the trail!" He fell swearing at his horse and sawed the bit across its mouth.

He shouted aloud with rage. "I will follow that trail, I tell you," he cried. "Where is the trail!"

He gripped the bridle of his prancing horse and searched amidst the grass. A long and clinging thread fell across his face, a gray streamer dropped about his bridle arm, some big, active thing with many legs ran down the back of his head. He looked up to discover one of those gray masses anchored as it were above him by these things and flapping out ends as a sail flaps when a boat comes about—but noiselessly.

He had an impression of many eyes, of a dense crew of

squat bodies, of long, many-jointed limbs hauling at their mooring ropes to bring the thing down upon him. For a space he stared up, reining in his prancing horse with the instinct born of years of horsemanship. Then the flat of a sword smote his back, and a blade flashed overhead and cut the drifting balloon of spider web free, and the whole mass lifted softly and drove clear and away.

"Spiders!" cried the voice of the gaunt man. "The things are full of big spiders! Look, my lord!"

The man with the silver bridle still followed the mass that drove away.

"Look, my lord!"

The master found himself staring down at a red smashed thing on the ground that, in spite of partial obliteration, could still wriggle unavailing legs. Then when the gaunt man pointed to another mass that bore down upon them, he drew his sword hastily. Up the valley now it was like a fog bank torn to rags. He tried to grasp the situation.

"Ride for it!" the little man was shouting. "Ride for it down the valley."

What happened then was like the confusion of a battle. The man with the silver bridle saw the little man go past him slashing furiously at imaginary cobwebs, saw him cannon into the horse of the gaunt man and hurl it and its rider to earth. His own horse went a dozen paces before he could rein it in. Then he looked up to avoid imaginary dangers, and then back again to see a horse rolling on the ground, the gaunt man standing and slashing over it at a rent and fluttering mass of gray that streamed and wrapped about them both. And thick and fast as thistledown on waste land on a windy day in July, the cobweb masses were coming on.

The little man had dismounted, but he dared not release his horse. He was endeavoring to lug the struggling brute back with the strength of one arm, while with the other he slashed aimlessly. The tentacles of a second gray mass had entangled themselves with the struggle, and this second gray mass came to its moorings, and slowly sank.

The master set his teeth, gripped his bridle, lowered his head and spurred his horse forward. The horse on the ground rolled over, there was blood and moving shapes upon the flanks, and the gaunt man suddenly leaving it, ran forward towards his master, perhaps ten paces. His legs were swathed and encumbered with gray; he made ineffectual movements with his sword. Gray streamers waved from him; there was a thin veil of gray across his face. With his left hand he beat at something on his body, and suddenly he stumbled and fell. He struggled to rise, and fell again, and suddenly, horribly, began to howl, "Oh—ohoo, ohooh!"

The master could see the great spiders upon him, and others upon the ground.

As he strove to force his horse nearer to this gesticulating screaming gray object that struggled up and down, there came a clatter of hooves, and the little man, in act of mounting, swordless, balanced on his belly athwart the white horse, and clutching its mane, whirled past. And again a clinging thread of gray gossamer swept across the master's face. All about him and over him, it seemed this drifting, noiseless cobweb circled and drew nearer him. . . .

To the day of his death he never knew just how the event of that moment happened. Did he, indeed, turn his horse, or did it really of its own accord stampede after its fellow? Suffice it that in another second he was galloping full tilt down the valley with his sword whirling furiously overhead. And all about him on the quickening breeze, the spiders' airships, their air bundles and air sheets, seemed to him to hurry in a conscious pursuit.

Clatter, clatter, thud, thud—the man with the silver bridle rode, heedless of his direction, with his fearful face looking up now right, now left, and his sword arm ready to slash. And a few hundred yards ahead of him, with a tail of torn cobweb trailing behind him, rode the little man on the white horse, still but imperfectly in the saddle. The reeds bent before them, the wind blew fresh and strong, over his shoulder the master could see the webs hurrying to overtake. . . .

He was so intent to escape the spiders' webs that only as his horse gathered together for a leap did he realize the ravine ahead. And then he realized it only to misunderstand and interfere. He was leaning forward on his horse's neck and sat up and back all too late.

But if in his excitement he had failed to leap, at any rate he had not forgotten how to fall. He was horseman again in midair. He came off clear with a mere bruise upon his shoulder, and his horse rolled, kicking spasmodic legs, and lay still. But the master's sword drove its point into the hard soil, and snapped clean across, as though Chance refused him any longer as her Knight, and the splintered end missed his face by an inch or so.

He was on his feet in a moment, breathlessly scanning the onrushing spider webs. For a moment he was minded to run, and then thought of the ravine, and turned back. He ran aside once to dodge one drifting terror, and then he was swiftly clambering down the precipitous sides, and out of the touch of the gale.

There under the lee of the dry torrent's steeper banks he might crouch, and watch these strange, gray masses pass and pass in safety till the wind fell, and it became possible to escape. And there for a long time he crouched, watching the strange, gray, ragged masses trail their streamers across his narrowed sky.

Once a stray spider fell into the ravine close beside him—a full foot it measured from leg to leg, and its body was half a man's hand—and after he had watched its monstrous alacrity of search and escape for a little while, and tempted it to bite his broken sword, he lifted up his iron heeled boot and smashed it into a pulp. He swore as he did so, and for a time sought up and down for another.

Then presently, when he was surer these spider swarms could not drop into the ravine, he found a place where he could sit down, and sat and fell into deep thought and began after his manner to gnaw his knuckles and bite his nails. And from this he was moved by the coming of the man with the white horse.

He heard him long before he saw him, as a clattering of hooves, stumbling footsteps, and a reassuring voice. Then the little man appeared, a rueful figure, still with a tail of white cobweb trailing behind him. They approached each other without speaking, without salutation. The little man was fatigued and shamed to the pitch of hopeless bitterness, and came to a stop at last, face to face with his seated master. The latter winced a little under his dependent's eye. "Well?" he said at last, with no pretense of authority.

"You left him!"

"My horse bolted."

"I know. So did mine."

He laughed at his master mirthlessly.

"I say my horse bolted," said the man who once had a silver-studded bridle.

"Cowards both," said the little man.

The other gnawed his knuckle through some meditative moments, with his eyes on his inferior.

"Don't call me a coward," he said at length.

"You are a coward like myself."

"A coward possibly. There is a limit beyond which every man must fear. That I have learnt at last. But not like yourself. That is where the difference comes in."

"I never could have dreamt you would have left him. He saved your life two minutes before. . . . Why are you our lord?"

The master gnawed his knuckles again, and his countenance was dark.

"No man calls me a coward," he said. "No. . . . A broken sword is better than none. . . . One spavined white horse cannot be expected to carry two men a four days' journey. I hate white horses, but this time it cannot be helped. You begin to understand me? . . . I perceive that you are minded, on the strength of what you have seen and fancy, to taint my reputation. It is men of your sort who unmake kings. Besides which—I never liked you."

"My lord!" said the little man.

"No," said the master. *"No!"*

He stood up sharply as the little man moved. For a minute perhaps they faced one another. Overhead the spiders' balls went driving. There was a quick movement among the pebbles; a running of feet, a cry of despair, a gasp and a blow. . . .

Towards nightfall the wind fell. The sun set in a calm serenity, and the man who had once possessed the silver bridle came at last very cautiously and by an easy slope out of the ravine again; but now he led the white horse that once belonged to the little man. He would have gone back to his horse to get his silver-mounted bridle again, but he feared night and a quickening breeze might still find him in the valley, and besides he disliked greatly to think he might discover his horse all swathed in cobwebs and perhaps unpleasantly eaten.

And as he thought of those cobwebs and of all the dangers he had been through, and the manner in which he had been preserved that day, his hand sought a little reliquary that hung about his neck, and he clasped it for a moment with heartfelt gratitude. As he did so his eyes went across the valley.

"I was hot with passion," he said, "and now she has met her reward. They also, no doubt—"

And behold! Far away out of the wooded slopes across the valley, but in the clearness of the sunset distinct and unmistakable, he saw a little spire of smoke.

At that his expression of serene resignation changed to an amazed anger. Smoke? He turned the head of the white horse about, and hesitated. And as he did so a little rustle of air went through the grass about him. Far away upon some reeds swayed a tattered sheet of gray. He looked at the cobwebs; he looked at the smoke.

"Perhaps, after all, it is not them," he said at last.

But he knew better.

After he had stared at the smoke for some time, he mounted the white horse.

As he rode, he picked his way amidst stranded masses of web. For some reason there were many dead spiders on the ground, and those that lived feasted guiltily on their fellow. At the sound of his horse's hooves they fled.

Their time had passed. From the ground, without either a wind to carry them or a winding sheet ready, these things, for all their poison, could do him no evil.

He flicked with his belt at those he fancied came too near. Once, where a number ran together over a bare place, he was minded to dismount and trample them with his boots, but this impulse he overcame. Ever and again he turned in his saddle, and looked back at the smoke.

"Spiders," he muttered over and over again. "Spiders! Well, well . . . . The next time I must spin a web."

WAZIAH

Joe R. Lansdale

The snow blew furiously, wound down through the peaks and canyons like a thick swathe of cold, wet gauze, wrapping the Black Hills tight in a Canadian-born blizzard. It was the first winter blow of 1874, and from the looks of things, a real icer.

Roland McArthur trudged through the knee-deep snow, stopped for a moment to get his bearings. He was leading his horse, Mick, and tied behind Mick was his pack mule, Clancy. He had given up riding old Mick an hour or so back. The blizzard had grown too thick and McArthur could see better down low than on horseback, so he had put on his snowshoes.

He was looking for a line shack. The same where he camped yearly on his fur-trapping run. He had come to the area none too soon: the blizzard had overtaken him without forewarning. One moment the sky was blue, the next nearly black, then it was full of churning snow.

What worried McArthur most was that the shack might not still be standing. It had been pretty ragged his last time passing, and unless some enterprising stop-over had lent work to it, it might well be a crumble of logs and stone now.

Whoever had built it in the first place had given up ownership, and it had not known extended habitation since. It was primarily an overnight stop for passing trappers, scouts, and mountain men. McArthur fit all those categories.

McArthur held tight to Mick's reins, cradled his Sharps rifle in his arms, and bent his head against the snow. He had tied his bandanna over his hat and beneath his chin. It kept his hat in place and lent a bit of warmth to his ears until the snow saturated the bandanna with wet and cold.

A short growl out of the blinding whiteness of the storm brought McArthur up short. He unslung his Sharps from his shoulder and held it at ready. The sound had not been unlike that of a grizzly. McArthur sniffed. He had lived in the mountains so long that his senses of smell and hearing were like those of an Indian. And there came to his nostrils, even through the wild blow of the snow, a thick cloying odor the likes of which he had never smelled. It was strong for only a moment, then gradually died on the wind.

McArthur cradled the rifle in his arms and moved forward again. Suddenly, a dark hulking thing wrapped in white loomed up before him. The shack. McArthur felt a tingle of relief in his belly, and lifting his legs high, he made short work of the distance between him and the cabin.

McArthur could smell smoke and meat cooking. Someone was inside. All the better. Company was a thing he needed. It would make the approaching night go faster.

"Hello, the shack," McArthur yelled in customary mountain greeting. The wind grabbed his voice and carried it away.

He slung his rifle over his shoulder and knocked on the thick plank door. No one answered, so he pounded. Still no one answered.

McArthur left the door and walked around to the side of the shack where, he remembered, a few of the logs were spaced well apart and uncaulked.

He discovered that someone had worked on the cabin since he had last seen it, yet there were still wide spaces here and there. As McArthur leaned forward to look inside he saw a flickering orange light. Then suddenly there was a scrabbling sound on the other side of the wall and a long, black thing was poking out of the chink and into his face.

McArthur threw up his arm and stumbled back. A rifle blast sent him flailing backwards into the snow.

Whiteness everywhere for a moment, then a journey down into a cold, black sea . . .

McArthur awoke and saw no angels. He saw first the flicker of fire and thought, "Uh-oh, the other place."

But no. He was comfortable, except for a slight headache, and he hardly felt the hellfires of eternal damnation.

McArthur blinked, brought his eyes into focus. Above him was a roof of log beams and split-log shingles. The roof seemed to tremble beneath the fury of the blizzard.

He sat up and looked toward the rock fireplace. That was where the glow was coming from—a warm, well-made fire. A grizzled old man sat by the fireplace on a hunk of log and looked at him—as ugly a geezer as McArthur had seen. The face was wrinkled like a sun-shriveled grape and dark as overdried leather. The man's eyes were black and so were most of the teeth showing through the salt-and-pepper beard. The old man had a Sharps rifle cradled in his arms and he was smiling, saying something that McArthur, still slightly addled, could not quite catch.

McArthur shook his head. That made it hurt. He touched his hand to his forehead and found a bandage there. Moaning, he lay back, realizing now that he was lying on a bundle of pelts.

The old man came to stand over him.

"You ain't hit bad, sonny. Threw your arm up just as I shot, hit my barrel, knocked off my aim. Just grazed your scalp a bit. Did a halfway bandage job on it. Sorry about that. I thought you was the thing."

"Thing?"

"Yeah, damn Wooly-Bugger."

McArthur had heard tales of the Wooly-Bugger. It was supposed to be some sort of huge beast that walked upright like a man, could imitate animals and birds, and had a stink that . . . McArthur remembered the strange odor he had smelled just before reaching the cabin.

"My horse . . . and mule?" McArthur asked.

"Ran off. Me, I'm on foot. Horse died a couple of days back. Hell, them critters ain't gone far. Not in this mess. And it's gettin' dark now. They'll be a wanderin' back . . . if the Wooly-Bugger don't get 'em."

McArthur sat up. "You mean grizzly?"

"Naw, I mean Wooly-Bugger. This ain't no grizz. It's been after us in the cabin all day long."

"Us?"

"Dauncy Injun gal and her papoose."

McArthur turned. Behind him, on a rickety bed of furs and pine boughs, an Indian girl lay, holding a bundle wrapped in fur to her breast. A cradle board lay next to her.

"Crow?" McArthur asked.

"She don't speak nothin' but a bit of Sioux. She ain't no kind of Injun I know. Least not right off. Flathead, maybe. She's a strange one. Can't look you right in the eye. Don't reckon her dough's done in the middle."

"You buy her someplace?"

"Naw. Ain't my woman. Found her here. I got here just before the blizzard hit, and then after that we had the Wooly-Bugger to mess with. He gets madder each time he comes back, and that damn, dauncy gal just sits there mumblin' to herself."

"It attacks the cabin?"

"Came prowlin' around right after I got here, finally started scratchin' at the door, and not like no damn puppy dog neither. Thought the door was gonna come off the hinges. I put a round through the top of the door and it moved on, but it didn't act like it was hurt none. Course that damn gal screechin' at the top of her lungs didn't do nothin' for my aim neither. It came back a couple of times after, sniffed around the place lookin' for a way in."

"You saw it?"

"Not good. It peeped in that hole over there, same where

I took a shot at you, and what I saw of it weren't like nothin' I'd ever seen before. Those eyes . . . like somethin' from hell, fella. Which reminds me. I don't rightly know your name."

"McArthur."

"McArthur, mine's Crawford. I call that gal Snowflake on account of I can't get nothin' out of her 'cept a few words of Sioux and ain't none of them words her name."

"Maybe she is Sioux."

"Maybe, but if so, she don't speak her own language none too good."

To McArthur she looked barely fifteen. She clutched the bundled baby to her chest tightly. Her eyes were like those of a frightened doe. McArthur thought her very beautiful.

He smiled at her, made a wavy sign with his hand; the sign of the snake, the symbol of the Sioux. It was his way of asking if she were Sioux.

For a moment she made no move. Then: "Heyah," she said softly. The Sioux word for no. Suddenly she looked away, seemingly no longer aware of McArthur or Crawford. She rocked back and forth from the waist, mumbling an incoherent melody.

"See?" Crawford said. "She ain't no Sioux, and she's some smarts, just like I told you. All I could get out of her is that she's from a tribe far away, and that she was stolen . . . Injuns, I guess. Said she learned Sioux from an older woman, a captive like her. Knows sign language pretty good. Anyway, she escaped and was running away. That's how she got here."

McArthur nodded.

"She don't have much to do with me, 'cept eatin' my food," Crawford said. "She takes care of that readily enough. Only person I ever saw that would eat my cookin' without chokin'. But hell, that ain't no compliment. I ain't cooked for no Injun before. They'll eat anything. I once saw some Digger Injuns eat grub worms out from under a rotten log."

"This Wooly-Bugger as you call it," McArthur said, his tone skeptical. "Think it's gone?"

"Hell, I don't know . . . you don't believe it's no Wooly-Bugger, do you?"

"I just reckon it's a bear."

Crawford smiled, went over to the fireplace and picked a pot of coffee from the edge of the fire. "Cup?"

McArthur nodded.

"I been in these mountains nigh on twenty years," Crawford said. "There's all sorts of things in here, things you wouldn't understand, less'n you seen them with your own eyes."

Crawford poured a cup and brought it to McArthur.

"There's Wooly-Buggers all right," Crawford continued. "Until now I've only seen sign of 'em. Them things is all through the Rockies, used to be thick with them, the Injuns say. They stretch all the way from here to Northern Californy. Injuns there call them Omah, and up farther north, Sasquatch. Supposed to be different types of 'em, but they all boil down to one thing, Wooly-Buggers.

"Them out toward Californy, if the Injuns can be believed, are a tamer variety. These here . . . well. Remember hearin' about them pilgrims from out East last year? That Monahan party?"

"Something about them," McArthur admitted. "Got killed by a bunch of grizzlies."

Crawford poured himself a cup of coffee and sipped. "You ain't never heard of no grizz pullin' a man's head off, have you? I don't mean claw it off, or bite it off. I mean pull it off, like it was a cork in a bottle. That's what happened to that Monahan man, leader of the bunch. His head was pulled off and thrown about thirty feet from where the rest of them lay. Them Wooly-Buggers scattered pilgrims all over the place."

McArthur finished off his coffee, sat the cup down . . . then suddenly he stood. It was the smell. The odor that had assaulted him outside earlier.

"Yeah," Crawford said, putting down his cup, picking up his Sharps. "I smell it too, boy. Your rifle and Colt's over there against the wall. I out and reloaded 'em for you."

McArthur moved for the Sharps, and as he reached to take it up, the caulking between the logs just above the rifle burst apart and a huge, hairy hand groped for him.

McArthur stumbled back as the claws reached out, flicking snow from their razor-sharp tips.

From behind him came the roar of Crawford's Sharps. A gout of blood leaped up from the waving arm of the beast, and suddenly the arm retreated into the night. Its disappearance was followed by a loud noise that was somewhere between a grizzly's growl and a puma's scream.

Then silence.

But only for a moment. Then came a sound like a hog rooting, then more like a grizzly grunting, and then there was a growl that shook the rafters of the cabin.

"Sonofabitch won't say quit," Crawford said.

By this time McArthur had gotten hold of his Sharps and had pushed the Colt into his belt. He looked at the Indian girl. She was hunkered over her baby, her eyes deep, dark pools of fear.

"Get away from the wall," McArthur warned the girl in Sioux.

"Waziah," she said, "Waziah. " McArthur recognized it as the Sioux word for Great God of the North.

And as if in response to her words, the wall shook with a powerful blow. A log creaked, sagged. Dirt and bark and mud caulking tumbled in, and then came the huge, hairy arms, heaving aside the logs, letting in the freezing outside air. Through the big rent in the wall McArthur could glimpse the beast. A behemoth nearly eight feet tall with eyes glowing like two falling stars.

The girl bent forward, almost out of its range. But one of the hands caught her long, black hair and jerked her back, causing the baby to fall from her arms and onto the bough bed.

McArthur fired at a spot between the glowing eyes. The beast tossed its head back in pain, roared. Its Bowie knife-sized teeth glinted in the glow of the firelight.

And then, fast as a panther, it was gone, and with it, right through the gap in the wall, the Indian girl Crawford called Snowflake.

But for a moment McArthur and Crawford were aware of only one thing, the whining baby on the bed. The furs had fallen away to reveal it.

It was only part human.

* * *

"It . . . it's a *thing*," Crawford said.

"Can't be . . . just can't be," McArthur said.

"Well, there that sucker is."

"How could a woman . . . and a beast that size . . . mate?"

"Must be a lot like the grizz. That old Wooly is built like a mountain, but I reckon he must be hung like a rabbit."

"My God," McArthur said after a time, "that's what the beast wanted. Its mate and child."

"Well, maybe we ought to put it out there where he can find it real easy like. If I'd known that's what he was after, I'd have given him Snowflake and her ugly little youngster long time back."

"Are you crazy? This . . . this baby is part human."

"Part Injun," Crawford said. "Well, now wait a minute. I think I see what you mean. Why, we could make us a bundle off this little sucker. Put him in one of them Wild West shows like they got goin' now. 'Come see the Beast of the Black Hills, taken at great risk of our lives . . . '"

"That's not what I meant at all. I mean it's part human, and that part is our concern. For that matter, I wouldn't turn a wild animal over to that thing."

"You ain't hintin' what I think you're hintin'?"

"I'm not hinting at all. I'm going after Snowflake."

"Yeah, well, write when you get time."

"And I'm taking this papoose with me, Crawford. I think it's got a better chance against the snow than me leaving it here with you."

"That's ugly talk, McArthur."

"Saying my opinion." McArthur picked up the screaming beast-child, looked at it closely. Its shape and face were human, but its body was covered with a thick gray fur. The eyes that looked up at him with a pleading expression were the eyes of Snowflake.

Bundling the baby up tight, so that it had only enough exposure to breathe, McArthur attached it to the cradle board.

"You're goin' out there?" Crawford said suddenly.

McArthur grunted that he was.

"Well, get the hell on out there then. You don't see me holdin' you back. I ain't goin' after that thing."

"Suit yourself." McArthur fastened the baby to his back by slipping his arms through the cradle board straps.

"Ain't that cute," Crawford said.

McArthur fastened on his snowshoes and picked up his rifle. Without a word he stepped through the hole in the cabin wall and out into the night.

The blizzard had stopped. There was a fair wind a-humming, but little snow came with it, just chill. The stars were out.

"You're gonna get your head popped off," Crawford yelled after McArthur.

McArthur began to trudge across the snow. The sign of the creature was obvious. Great tracks, looking more like the prints of snowshoes than of men, wound off toward the tall trees; thick, blue black shadows in the moonlight.

The little creature on McArthur's back whined softly, then was silent. McArthur found himself wondering if the child was male or female. The whole thing had happened so fast he had not had time to speculate on anything. He could only guess that these beasts, being some sort of near-humans, stole their mates from Indian tribes, or perhaps some of the more superstitious bands offered the women in tribute to the creatures, thinking them some sort of gods. What had Snowflake said? "Waziah." Great God of the North.

It was certainly true that the Sioux often dressed up in the skins of animals, the bear for instance, and danced in a manner that led most to believe they were offering tribute to the strength of the beast. Could it be that their dances were not to the bear at all, that the outfits they wore were in fact representative of the Wooly-Buggers, as Crawford called them? Could it be the dances were more than a tribute to the creature's strength? Perhaps it was all part of a ritual to appease the beasts and keep them away? The offering of women could well be another part of the ritual, something no white man's eyes had seen.

"Wait the hell up!"

McArthur stopped in his tracks and turned. Crawford was puffing his way across the snow, his snowshoes throwing up little clouds of white in the moonlight.

"I ain't stayin' in that rickety cabin. Not with that thing out here. I'd just as soon have me some company out under the stars when it pulls my head off and spits down my windpipe."

McArthur nodded, turned back to following the tracks. They had not gone far when they found McArthur's mule, Clancy. Its head had been twisted around at an odd angle. The supplies that had been strapped to its back were tossed about and partially covered by snow.

Not far from where Clancy lay, they found what was left

of Mick. The animal's head was gone and generous portions of meat had been ripped from its rump.

"Had him a snack," Crawford said.

McArthur clenched the Sharps, turned back to following the tracks. Crawford came close behind.

The forest grew thick about them, and had the great beast not gone before them, slapping down brush and uprooting trees, clearing a path for itself, it would have been hard going indeed. Now, in fact, the path was easy to follow. Too easy, thought McArthur, but by that time they had come to the end of the trail. Thick trees lay in front of them and on either side.

"You thinkin' what I'm thinkin'?" Crawford said.

"I'm thinking it laid a mighty easy trail to follow, and now it's gone into the woods and is doubling back."

"Figures we can't move through the trees as well as it can."

"Probably figures right. Big as it is, it still moves like a ghost."

"Nearby, I reckon. I think maybe we ought to do a fast melt before . . ."

But it was too late. Suddenly a small spruce crashed down on McArthur's left, whipped across and knocked Crawford off his feet. And there was the beast.

It didn't have Snowflake with it, just its naked fury. It stood eight feet tall. Saliva dripped from its knifelike teeth and its eyes were fiery points of hate. Its odor was overwhelming. A small spot of red glistened on the beast's forehead where McArthur had shot it earlier. It looked no worse than his own wounded forehead.

McArthur jerked up his Sharps and fired. He thought he had at least hit the creature's right shoulder, but it stepped forward anyway, took hold of McArthur by the head and started to lift.

Crawford rolled to his feet, lifted his rifle and fired at the back of the thing's head. "Take that!" he yelled. The shot was on target, but the thick fur, flesh, and bone stopped the 550-grain bullet as if it were a gnat. It was a shot that would have dropped a grizzly or a bull buffalo dead in its tracks.

But it only got the creature's attention. It wheeled, dropped McArthur and went for Crawford. Crawford dove for the thicket, squirmed his way into the brush.

The creature stepped forward, and grasping a pair of small pines in the crook of either arm, uprooted them and tossed them aside.

Crawford scrambled back farther into the brush, crawling on hands and knees, dragging the Sharps after him.

McArthur stumbled to his feet and attempted to pull his pistol from his belt. His Sharps lay somewhere in the snow. He had the Colt worked loose when the creature turned back to him.

McArthur fired twice. The bullets could have been fleas for all the creature noticed them. Turning to run, McArthur found that he could not get through the thick trees. The cradle board held him.

The beast reached for him, took hold of the cradle board and ripped it free of McArthur's back. McArthur kept moving forward, into the trees. The creature held the cradle board high above its head, and raising its angry face to the heavens, bellowed like a bull buffalo, loud enough to shake down the moon.

Turning, holding the child gently beneath one arm, the beast swatted aside trees and brush, made a new path for itself, disappeared into the gloom.

McArthur recovered his rifle and reloaded. He replaced the bullets in his revolver, looked down the jagged trail of broken trees and trampled brush, watched the darkness where he had last seen the beast.

"A mite bad-tempered, ain't he?" Crawford said, edging out of the trees.

McArthur ignored him, started in the direction the creature had gone.

"Hey," Crawford said. "Give it up."

McArthur kept moving forward, traveling at a half-trot now. Cursing, Crawford began to follow.

They had not gone far when they found Snowflake. She stumbled out of the trees and into McArthur's arms. Immediately she began to scream and fight, but after a moment she realized it was McArthur and not the creature.

In Sioux McArthur asked her what had happened. She quickly explained in broken Sioux that the beast had reached her into the uppermost branches of a small pine, and then, tearing all the lower branches off, had deserted her, probably intending to come back for her later. Snowflake had managed to jump into a snowbank. The next thing she knew she was stumbling into McArthur's arms. But the one thing that concerned her most was her child.

Grimly McArthur told her, gestured to where the creature had disappeared. In the next instant Snowflake was running, and McArthur and Crawford ran with her.

The creature was easy to follow for a while. It had made no effort to hide its trail. Its massive footprints were everywhere, as were uprooted and knocked-aside trees. But soon they came to a clearing where the trees ended and the bare rocks tumbled off and down into what seemed like blue black infinity.

"I don't like the looks of this place none," Crawford said. "That blessed thing is smart. Woods behind us, canyon in front of us, narrow rock path left and right. . . . Naw, I don't like it at all. Could be another trap."

McArthur had bent down close to the ground to look for a sign. Even in the moonlight he could see none.

"Could have gone either way," McArthur said. "I think we should spread out. You go left, we'll go right. You game?"

Crawford shook his head, but said, "Ah, why the hell not. I ain't been actin' much smarter than a pig's ass up till now, so why not get et like one?"

McArthur took Snowflake's arm and they went right. Crawford went left, moving along the edge of the canyon rim.

The sky was clouding up again, covering the moon so that it looked like a filmed-over eye. McArthur looked to his left, looked out into the darkness of the canyon, thought of the forever-fall down and shivered.

After a while of moving at a fast trot, McArthur stopped to examine for a sign again. There was none that he could see. He decided that the creature had most likely gone the other direction.

* * *

Crawford couldn't believe his luck. He found the cradle board complete with baby before he had gone a hundred yards. It hung from a low limb where the creature had wrapped one of the straps about it. The furs had come undone around the little creature's face and Crawford could see its features distinctly. It looked much more human to him at a second glance.

Unfastening the cradle board, Crawford whispered, "You're gonna make me rich, little critter."

Crawford tied one of the straps back together and swung it over his left shoulder, leaving his gun arm free. "Tough luck, McArthur. I'm headin' for the Wild West show."

As Crawford moved off he saw huge footprints in the snow. The creature was circling back, moving toward where McArthur and Snowflake were.

Crawford considered the situation for a moment, then said aloud, "I didn't want to go chasin' after no damn Injun in the first place."

Turning, Crawford started away from the tracks.

McArthur and Snowflake were about to turn back down the trail when they heard a voice saying repeatedly, "Take that, take that, take that, take that . . ." It was Crawford's voice, and it sounded as if he had gone plumb loco.

"Come," McArthur said. "*Hoppo!*"

"Take that, take that, take that, take that," the voice continued.

McArthur moved toward the sound, Snowflake trailing close behind. A ridge of snow lay before them; at its crest were two stubby pines. The voice seemed to be coming from there, or just over the rise.

Upwards McArthur went, over the snow-covered rocks. Snowflake came on close behind him.

And suddenly the snow between the two scrubby pines burst upwards and expanded . . . and proved to not be snow at all, but the creature.

McArthur understood too late. The voice had been the creature's. It had merely imitated Crawford's words back when it first ambushed them, imitated them in the way it imitated other animals. Then, crouching down against the snow, blending in, it had waited.

The beast raised its arms high above its head, a great stone in its hands. The stone flew as if launched from a catapult. McArthur stepped nimbly aside, but the stone hit Snowflake in the chest, carried her back and down the ridge. She hit on her back, and still clutching the stone, she began to roll. Head over heels she went, right over the edge of the cliff and out into the maw of the canyon, down into pitch blackness.

She screamed once.

The creature screamed as if in anguish.

"Bastard," McArthur yelled, and he brought up the Sharps. He avoided aiming for the head. He had learned his lesson there. The rifle went off and the shot hit the creature in the throat.

The beast gurgled, stumbled back, but regained its footing. It looked more furious than hurt. Flashing its huge teeth in the weak moonlight, it came charging down the rise.

McArthur grabbed the Sharps by the barrel and flung it. It bounced off the creature's chest like a twig, didn't slow the beast at all.

The creature swung its razor-sharp claws.

McArthur tried to step back, but the snowshoes sent him off balance. He couldn't quite get away from the claws. They ripped across his chest, sending waves of agony through his body. The snow in front of him was suddenly sprinkled with red.

McArthur dropped to one knee.

The beast raised its huge arm for another swipe, when abruptly thunder filled the air and the beast threw back its head and screamed.

Crawford, the baby still slung on the cradle board across his left shoulder, stood at the top of the rise, his Sharps pointed down. His shot had hit the creature in the small of the back and penetrated deeply, but not deep enough.

The beast turned, and as before was attracted to its immediate tormenter. It began climbing the rise at a run.

Crawford drew his revolver, and as the beast climbed upwards, stumbling a bit now, he took steady aim and fired a shot directly into the creature's left eye. The animal's head jerked back.

"Come and get it, Wooly-Bugger," Crawford snarled. In rapid succession he emptied his revolver into the beast. But still it came.

Crawford dropped the cradle board off his arm, tossed aside his revolver and drew his Bowie. The creature grabbed at him, but Crawford avoided the arms, jumped straight into the creature. He grasped the thick fur at the creature's chest with one hand, locked his legs around its waist. With the other hand he drove the Bowie into the beast repeatedly. It was like trying to stick a needle through a half-dozen bear hides lumped together.

The beast clutched Crawford to its chest, began to squeeze. Crawford's hands were now pinned and he could no longer strike. His brain filled with the awful odor of the creature and he began to fall away into darkness.

McArthur, seeing through a haze, drew his revolver and half-stumbled, half-ran up the rise. When he was less than six feet away he began to fire into the creature, hitting in and around the wound Crawford had made in the small of the thing's back.

The creature staggered, dropped Crawford. Crawford rolled halfway down the rise and stopped rolling. He didn't move.

The beast turned slowly to face McArthur and his empty revolver. Blood covered its face, dripped off its fur. Even in the cloudy moonlight, McArthur could see that one eye was gone.

The creature roared, staggered.

McArthur pushed two shells into the revolver, but before he could fire the beast stumbled back and fell, landing directly on top of the cradle board, driving it deep into the snow.

McArthur went down to Crawford. The man was breathing but it sounded like wind whistling through a hollow rock. McArthur knew as well as Crawford that ribs had punctured a lung.

Crawford grinned with his black, now bloodstained teeth. "Should of went ahead and run off," he said. "Could of made a lot of money . . . Wild West Show. But . . . but you're a mountain man, same . . . same as me."

And then the life went out of Crawford's eyes.

* * *

High up there in the Black Hills McArthur left them to the wind, the sky, the sun, the snow—where their bones would mingle with those of all the other creatures of the wild Dakotas.

THE SPECTRE BRIDE

Anonymous

The winter nights up at Sault Ste. Marie are as white and luminous as the Milky Way. The silence that rests upon the solitude appears to be white also. Nature has included sound in her arrestment. Save the still white frost, all things are obliterated. The stars are there, but they seem to belong to heaven and not to earth. They are at an immeasurable height, and so black is the night that the opaque ether rolls between them and the observer in great liquid billows.

In such a place it is difficult to believe that the world is peopled to any great extent. One fancies that Cain has just killed Abel, and that there is need for the greatest economy in the matter of human life.

The night Ralph Hagadorn started out for Echo Bay he felt as if he were the only man in the world, so complete was the solitude through which he was passing. He was going over to attend the wedding of his best friend, and was, in fact, to act as the groomsman. Business had delayed him, and he was compelled to make his journey at night. But he hadn't gone far before he began to feel the exhilaration of the skater. His skates were keen, his legs fit for a longer journey than the one he had undertaken, and the tang of the frost was to him what a spur is to a spirited horse.

He cut through the air as a sharp stone cleaves the water. He could feel the tumult of the air as he cleft it. As he went on he began to have fancies. It seemed to him that he was enormously tall—a great Viking of the Northland, hastening over icy fiords to his love. That reminded him that he had a love—though, indeed, that thought was always present with him as a background for other thoughts. To be sure, he had not told her she was his love, because he had only seen her a few times and the opportunity had not presented itself. She lived at Echo Bay, too, and was to be the maid of honor to his friend's bride—which was another reason why he skated on almost as swiftly as the wind, and why, now and then, he let out a shout of exhilaration.

The one drawback in the matter was that Marie Beaujeu's father had money, and that Marie lived in a fine house and wore otter skin about her throat and little satin-lined mink boots on her feet when she went sledding, and that the jacket in which she kept a bit of her dead mother's hair had a black pearl in it as big as a pea. These things made it difficult—nay, impossible—for Ralph Hagadorn to say anything more than "I love you." But that much he meant to have the satisfaction of saying, no matter what came of it.

With this determination growing upon him he swept along the ice which gleamed under the starlight. Indeed, Venus made a glowing path toward the west and seemed to reassure him. He was sorry he could not skim down that avenue of light from the love star, but he was forced to turn his back upon it and face toward the northeast.

It came to him with a shock that he was not alone. His eyelashes were a good deal frosted and his eyeballs blurred with the cold, and at first he thought it an illusion. But he rubbed his eyes hard and at length made sure that not very far in front of him was a long white skater in fluttering garments who sped over the snows fast as ever werewolf went. He called aloud, but there was no answer, and then he gave chase, setting his teeth hard and putting a tension on his firm young muscles. But however fast he might go the white skater went faster. After a time he became convinced, as he chanced to glance for a second at the North Star, that the white skater was leading him out of his direct path. For a moment he hesitated, wondering if he should not keep to his road, but the strange companion seemed to draw him on irresistibly, and so he followed.

Of course it came to him more than once that this might be no earthly guide. Up in those latitudes men see strange things when the hoar frost is on the earth. Hagadorn's father, who lived up there with the Lake Superior Indians and worked in the copper mines, had once welcomed a woman at his hut on a bitter night who was gone by morning, and who left wolf tracks in the snow—yes, it was so, and John Fontanelle, the half-breed, could tell you about it any day—if he were alive. (Alack, the snow where the wolf tracks were is melted now!)

Well, Hagadorn followed the white skater all the night, and when the ice flushed red at dawn and arrows of lovely light shot up into the cold heavens, she was gone, and Hagadorn was at his destination. Then, as he took off his skates while the sun climbed arrogantly up to his place above all other things, Hagadorn chanced to glance lakeward, and he saw there was a great wind-rift in the ice and that the waves showed blue as sapphires beside the gleaming ice. Had he swept along his intended path, watching the stars to guide him, his glance turned upward, all his body at magnificent momentum, he must certainly have gone into that cold grave. The white skater had been his guardian angel!

Much impressed, he went up to his friend's house, expecting to find there the pleasant wedding furore. But someone met him quietly at the door, and his friend came downstairs to greet him with a solemn demeanor.

"Is this your wedding face?" cried Hagadorn. "Why, really, if this is the way you are affected, the sooner I take warning the better."

"There's no wedding today," said his friend.

"No wedding? Why, you're not—"

"Marie Beaujeu died last night—"

"Marie—"

"Died last night. She had been skating in the afternoon, and she came home chilled and wandering in her mind, as if the frost had got in it somehow. She got worse and worse and talked all the time of you."

"Of me?"

"We wondered what it all meant. We didn't know you were lovers."

"I didn't know it myself; more's the pity."

"She said you were on the ice. She said you didn't know about the big breaking up, and she cried to us that the wind was off shore. Then she cried that you could come in by the old French Creek if you only knew—"

"I came in that way," interrupted Hagadorn.

"How did you come to do that? It's out of your way."

So Hagadorn told him how it came to pass.

And that day they watched beside the maiden, who had tapers at her head and feet, and over in the little church the bride who might have been at her wedding said prayers for her friend. Then they buried her in her bridesmaid's white, and Hagadorn was there before the altar with her, as he intended from the first. At midnight the day of the burial her friends were married in the gloom of the cold church, and they walked together through the snow to lay their bridal wreaths on her grave.

Three nights later Hagadorn started back again to his home. They wanted him to go by sunlight, but he had his way and went when Venus made her bright path on the ice. He hoped for the companionship of the white skater. But he did not have it. His only companion was the wind. The only voice he heard was the baying of a wolf on the north shore. The world was as white as if it had just been created and the sun had not yet colored nor man defiled it.

FARM

BLOODY POLLY

Michael Norman and Beth Scott

Frances Clara Brown was a strikingly beautiful woman. Tall
and slender at age eighteen with a sweet disposition and gentle
face, she had flaxen hair that framed a creamy complexion set off
by large, expressive brown eyes. She lived with her father,
Frederick Brown, her mother and brothers and sisters in a log
cabin a few miles from Lancaster, in Garrard County. Mr. Brown
had brought his family to the rough Kentucky wilderness from
Maryland in 1815.

He soon turned their frontier cabin and few acres into a
large, thriving plantation. His mules broke the earth for crops,
and a mill built with his own hands separated hemp from flax for
spinning.

Life was good until the day Harry Geiss showed up.

Now Frances Clara had a sister, Polly, two years her

elder. With black hair, flashing eyes, and a fiery temper, she usually got her way.

Polly's worst fear was becoming an "old maid." Women usually married by their late teens in that era, so her prospects were already looking dim.

When Harry Geiss came along—single and evidently on his way to becoming a prosperous merchant—Polly Brown set her sights upon him. They became engaged, but it wasn't long before his attentions turned toward her younger sister, Frances Clara. Perhaps Polly's temper made the young bachelor have second thoughts. But it was soon evident to everyone in the neighborhood that handsome Harry Geiss would soon marry vivacious "Fanny Clary" Brown.

Apparent to all, that is, except Polly Brown.

She was enraged at the thought of losing Harry Geiss to her sister. Her devious mind created a scheme so horrible that years passed before its full impact was known.

The fateful series of events began one morning when the merchant Geiss set out for Maysville, Kentucky, on the Ohio River. There was no transportation to the deep wilderness surrounding Lancaster, so goods were transported from Philadelphia to Maysville, where they were off-loaded and toted to the outlying pioneer communities. Geiss periodically made the several-hundred-mile round-trip, taking several days to complete the journey. On this day, however, as he bade farewell to Frances Clara, he had no way of knowing that it would be the last time the two would ever be together.

A few hours after Geiss's departure, Polly Brown found her sister weaving. Polly cheerfully persuaded her sister to accompany her to a Mrs. Brassfield's, there to examine a new quilt pattern the woman was completing. The two young women plunged through the thick forest. In a grove of papaw trees Polly remarked that Frances Clara's hair was coming loose. She would pin it up, she said, guiding her sister to a log.

Frances Clara should never have turned her back. As soon as she did, Polly Brown drew a hatchet from beneath her skirts and, grasping her sister's hair firmly in her left hand, brought the sharpened blade down in a mighty swing at her sister's pale neck.

Blood spewed from severed arteries. *Chop . . . chop . . . chop.* Blow after blow rained down on helpless Frances Clara, her sister crazily swinging the bloody hatchet in a murderous rage. Frances Clara cried out for mercy, but her screams were quickly silenced. Polly didn't stop until her sister's mangled head rolled off her lifeless torso.

The murder had been carefully planned, savagely executed. Polly Brown had picked a particular part of the forest in which to carry out her deed. She dragged her sister's remains to a nearby sinkhole and buried them in the soft earth, being careful to obliterate any signs of a struggle or blood. So meticulous had been her scheme that she had secreted a change of clothing nearby so as not to call attention to her own bloodstained garments.

In a field some distance away, three young slaves—Abe, Tom, and Pomp—heard Frances Clara's screams. "Polly, don't kill me!" she cried. Abe, the oldest, dashed forward and hid behind a bush. He saw Polly inflict the final, mortal wounds. Quickly fleeing, he told his companions what he had seen. He made them swear never to reveal what had occurred. All three were fearful they would be blamed for the murder.

For the rest of the day, Polly Brown quietly gathered up her sister's saddle, good clothing, and personal effects from their home and stashed them in another area of the forest several hundred yards away from her sister's dismal grave. She calmly returned home and awaited the discovery of Frances Clara's absence. The murderess had an explanation for that prepared, too.

As twilight descended, Frances Clara's parents did indeed wonder where their daughter was. Polly slyly stepped forward and offered the opinion that she must have run away with Harry Geiss as he had left for Maysville that morning. She pointed to the fact that Frances Clara's saddle and "Sunday clothes" were missing, sure signs that Geiss had persuaded her to leave with him. The hint of a self-satisfied smile must have slipped across Polly's face. She knew that it would be days or weeks before Geiss returned with his merchandise. By that time, she hoped, her rival would have been forgotten and Harry Geiss would turn his attention to her.

Polly Brown's plan would have succeeded but for a macabre discovery by several small boys a few weeks later. Sent to gather papaws in the woods, Claiborne Lear, Joshua Comely, and Sammy Johnson were startled by a wild pig chewing at something on the ground. When they got closer, they were scared witless to see that the pig's snack was actually a thin, white hand sticking out of the sandy soil.

The boys raced home to tell their parents of the awful discovery. Within hours, several dozen neighbors had gathered at the papaw patch. They unearthed the remains of the headless Frances Clara Brown. Her parents reburied her on the plantation grounds.

The whereabouts of Frances Clara's good clothing and saddle puzzled the Brown family. A psychic, a man named Ramsey who lived in nearby Lancaster, predicted that the missing items would be found precisely 440 yards south of the Brown home. Family friend Thompson Arnold measured out the distance and found the material only a few inches below ground.

The devious plan hatched by Polly Brown succeeded in keeping anyone from suspecting her, but failed at winning Harry Geiss's affection. He eventually left town.

The owners of the slaves grew suspicious. They recalled that the youths had been working near where Polly's body was found. Eventually, Tom and Pomp were arrested and jailed. Perhaps someone overheard one of them talking about the murder, or maybe they were confused by Abe's orders to keep quiet. Whatever the reason, they were tried for murder. The only evidence was presented by their jailer, who claimed to have heard one of them say, "The first lick didn't kill her."

Justice was nonexistent for African-American slaves, and any pretense of fairness a mockery. The boys were found guilty on December 13, 1820. Tom was hanged on January 7, 1821. Pomp was sent to the gallows two weeks later. Nothing is known of Abe's fate.

Polly Brown didn't raise a hand to prevent the tragic hanging of two innocent young men. The blood of three persons now stained her hands.

It was all too much even for the twisted mind of Polly

Brown. Her family moved away to Indianapolis, leaving only her behind. It isn't known why. Perhaps it was her turning toward herbs as cures for disease, or her long walks in the woods—particularly near the old papaw trees where her sister's body lay for so long.

She moved into a small cabin when the Brown farm was purchased by Josiah Burnside. Mr. and Mrs. Logan Harris lived there and more or less looked after her.

One night many years later, Polly Brown was returning through the wood after a visit with a sick "patient." Her herbal medicines were popular on the frontier, where a physician might be hundreds of miles distant. On this evening, however, even the strongest drugs would not have helped her. Coming at her was the ghost of Frances Clara, her arms outstretched as if to grab at her tormentor. The apparition's neck was a bloody stump.

Polly turned and ran, shaking uncontrollably at the sight of her reanimated sister. When she stumbled into the Harris cabin babbling about Frances Clara's ghost, the couple immediately put her to bed. From that night forward, Polly Brown descended into a mania from which she never recovered. Eventually she was chained to her bed after she was caught attempting to break into her old home. Her gray hair fell in long, unkempt strands about her shoulders; her once dancing eyes grew dull and sunken. Mr. and Mrs. Harris could only keep her in a rough-sewn sack dress.

The truth was eventually learned. As she lay dying, Polly Brown confessed to the murder of her sister, and expressed her sorrow for the wrongful deaths of Pomp and Tom. She amazed Mr. and Mrs. Harris by appearing completely lucid on her deathbed.

Josiah Burnside and his wife Almira raised a large family on the old Brown plantation. Regular appearances by the ghost of Frances Clara became a part of the family's tradition. She would playfully pull covers from the bed or rush through the front door, slamming it as she entered. The soft rustle of her skirts could be heard ascending the stairs to her old loom room.

THE FACELESS THING

Edward D. Hoch

Sunset: golden flaming clouds draped over distant canyons barely seen in the dusk of the dying day; farmland gone to rot; fields in the foreground given over wildly to the running of the rabbit and the woodchuck; the farmhouse gray and paint-peeled, sleeping possibly but more likely dead—needing burial.

It hadn't changed much in all those years. It hadn't changed; only died.

He parked the car and got out, taking it all in with eyes still intent and quick for all their years. Somehow he hadn't really thought it would still be standing. Farmhouses that were near collapse fifty years ago shouldn't still be standing; not when all the people, his mother and father and aunt and the rest, were all long in their graves.

He was an old man, had been an old man almost as long

as he could remember. Youth to him was only memories of this farm, so many years before, romping in the hay with his little sister at his side; swinging from the barn ropes, exploring endless dark depths out beyond the last field. After that, he was old—through misty college days and marriage to a woman he hadn't loved, through a business and political career that carried him around the world. And never once in all those years had he journeyed back to this place, this farmhouse now given over to the weeds and insects. They were all dead; there was no reason to come back . . . no reason at all.

Except the memory of the ooze.

A childhood memory, a memory buried with the years, forgotten sometimes but always there, crowded into its own little space in his mind, was ready to confront him and startled him with its vividness.

The ooze was a place beyond the last field, where water always collected in the springtime and after a storm; water running over dirt and clay and rock, merging with the soil until there was nothing underfoot but a black ooze to rise above your boots. He'd followed the stream rushing with storm water, followed it to the place where it cut into the side of the hill.

It was the memory of the tunnel, really, that had brought him back—the dark tunnel leading nowhere, gurgling with rain-fed water, barely large enough for him to fit through. A tunnel floored with unseen ooze, peopled by unknown danger; that was a place for every boy.

Had he been only ten that day? Certainly he'd been no more than eleven, leading the way while his nine-year-old sister followed. "This way. Be careful of the mud." She'd been afraid of the dark, afraid of what they might find there. But he'd called encouragement to her; after all, what could there be in all this ooze to hurt them?

How many years? Fifty?

"What *is* it, Buddy?" She'd always called him Buddy. What is it, Buddy? Only darkness, and a place maybe darker than dark, with a half-formed shadow rising from the ooze. He'd brought along his father's old lantern, and he fumbled to light it.

"Buddy!" she'd screamed—just once—and in the flare of the match he'd seen the thing, great and hairy and covered with ooze; something that lived in the darkness here, something that hated the light. In that terrifying instant it had reached out for his little sister and pulled her into the ooze.

That was the memory, a memory that came to him sometimes only at night. It had pursued him down the years like a fabled hound, coming to him, reminding him, when all was well with the world. It was like a personal demon sent from Hades to torture him. He'd never told anyone about that thing in the ooze, not even his mother. They'd cried and carried on when his sister was found the next day, and they'd said she'd drowned. He was not one to say differently.

And the years had passed. For a time, during his high school days, he read the local papers—searching for some word of the thing, some veiled news that it had come out of that forgotten cavern. But it never did; it liked the dark and damp too much. And, of course, no one else ever ventured into the stream bed. That was a pursuit only for the very young and very foolish.

By the time he was twenty, the memory was fading,

merging with other thoughts, other goals, until at times he thought it only a child's dream. But then at night it would come again in all its vividness, and the thing in the ooze would beckon him.

A long life, long and crowded . . . One night he'd tried to tell his wife about it, but she wouldn't listen. That was the night he'd realized how little he'd ever loved her. Perhaps he'd only married her because, in a certain light, she reminded him of that sister of his youth. But the love that sometimes comes later came not at all to the two of them. She was gone now, like his youth, like his family and friends. There was only this memory remaining. The memory of a thing in the ooze.

Now the weeds were tall, beating against his legs, stirring nameless insects to flight with every step. He pressed a handkerchief against his brow, sponging the sweat that was forming there. Would the dark place still be there, or had fifty years of rain and dirt sealed it forever?

"Hello there," a voice called out. It was an old voice, barely carrying with the breeze. He turned and saw someone on the porch of the deserted farmhouse. An old woman, ancient and wrinkled.

"Do I know you?" he asked, moving closer.

"You may," she answered. "You're Buddy, aren't you? My, how old I've gotten. I used to live at the next farm, when you were just a boy. I was young then myself. I remember you."

"Oh! Mrs. . . . ?" The name escaped him, but it wasn't important.

"Why did you come back, Buddy? Why, after all these years?"

He was an old man. Was it necessary to explain his actions to this woman from the past? "I just wanted to see the place," he answered. "Memories, you know."

"Bitter memories. Your little sister died here, did she not?" The old woman should have been dead, should have been dead and in her grave long ago.

He paused in the shade of the porch roof. "She died here, yes, but that was fifty years ago."

"How old we grow, how ancient! Is that why you returned?"

"In a way. I wanted to see the spot."

"Ah! The little brook back there beyond the last field. Let me walk that way with you. These old legs need exercise."

"Do you live here?" he asked, wanting to escape her now but knowing not how.

"No, still down the road. All alone now. Are you all alone, too?"

"I suppose so." The high grass made walking difficult.

"You know what they all said at the time, don't you? They all said you were fooling around, like you always did, and pushed her into the water."

There was a pain in his chest from breathing so hard. He was an old man. "Do you believe that?"

"What does it matter?" she answered. "After all these fifty years, what does it matter?"

"Would you believe me," he began, then hesitated into silence. Of course she wouldn't believe him, but he had to tell now. "Would you believe me if I told you what happened?"

* * *

She was a very old woman and she panted to keep up even his slow pace. She was ancient even to his old eyes, even in his world where now everyone was old. "I would believe you," she said.

"There was something in the ooze. Call it a monster, a demon, if you want. I saw it in the light of a match, and I can remember it as if it were yesterday. It took her."

"Perhaps," she said.

"You don't believe me."

"I said I would. This sun is hot today, even at twilight."

"It will be gone soon. I hate to hurry you, old woman, but I must reach the stream before dark."

"The last field is in sight."

Yes, it was in sight. But how would he ever fit through that small opening, how would he face the thing, even if by some miracle it still waited there in the ooze? Fifty years was a long long time.

"Wait here," he said as they reached the little stream at last. It hadn't changed much, not really.

"You won't find it." He lowered his aged body into the bed of the stream, feeling once again the familiar forgotten ooze closing over his shoes.

"No one has to know," she called after him. "Even if there was something, that was fifty years ago."

But he went on, to the place where the water vanished into the rock. He held his breath and groped for the little flashlight in his pocket. Then he ducked his head and followed the water into the black.

It was steamy here, steamy and hot with the sweat of the

earth. He flipped on the flashlight with trembling hands and followed its narrow beam with his eyes. The place was almost like a room in the side of the hill, a room perhaps seven feet high, with a floor of mud and ooze that seemed almost to bubble as he watched.

"Come on," he said softly, almost to himself. "I know you're there. You've got to be there."

And then he saw it, rising slowly from the ooze. A shapeless thing without a face, a thing that moved so slowly it might have been dead. An old, very old thing. For a long time he watched it, unable to move, unable to cry out. And even as he watched, the thing settled back softly into the ooze, as if even this small exertion had tired it.

"Rest," he said, very quietly. "We are all so old now."

And then he made his way back out of the cave, along the stream, and finally pulled himself from the clinging ooze. The ancient woman was still waiting on the bank, with fireflies playing about her in the dusk.

"Did you find anything?" she asked him.

"Nothing," he answered.

"Fifty years is a long time. You shouldn't have come back."

He sighed and fell into step beside her. "It was something I had to do."

"Come up to my house, if you want. I can make you a bit of tea."

His breath was coming better now, and the distance back to the farmhouse seemed shorter than he'd remembered. "I think I'd like that," he said. . . .

EXOTIC

ALLAL

Paul Bowles

He was born in the hotel where his mother worked. The hotel had only three dark rooms which gave on a courtyard behind the bar. Beyond was another smaller patio with many doors. This was where the servant lived, and where Allal spent his childhood.

The Greek who owned the hotel had sent Allal's mother away. He was indignant because she, a girl of fourteen, had dared to give birth while she was working for him. She would not say who the father was, and it angered him to reflect that he himself had not taken advantage of the situation while he had had the chance. He gave the girl three months' wages and told her to go home to Marrakech. Since the cook and his wife liked the girl and offered to let her live with them for a while, he agreed that she might stay on until the baby was big enough to travel. She remained in the back patio for a few months with the cook and his wife, and then one day she disappeared, leaving the baby behind. No one heard of her again.

As soon as Allal was old enough to carry things, they set him to work. It was not long before he could fetch a pail of water from the well behind the hotel. The cook and his wife were childless, so that he played alone.

When he was somewhat older he began to wander over the empty tableland outside. There was nothing else up here but the barracks, and they were enclosed by a high blind wall of red adobe. Everything else was below in the valley: the town, the gardens, and the river winding southward among the thousands of palm trees. He could sit on a point of rock far above and look down at the people walking in the alleys of the town. It was only later that he visited the place and saw what the inhabitants were like. Because he had been left behind by his mother they called him a son of sin, and laughed when they looked at him. It seemed to him that in this way they hoped to make him into a shadow, in order not to have to think of him as real and alive. He awaited with dread the time when he would have to go each morning to the town and work. For the moment he helped in the kitchen and served the officers from the barracks, along with the few motorists who passed through the region. He got small tips in the restaurant, and free food and lodging in a cell of the servants' quarters, but the Greek gave him no wages. Eventually he reached an age when this situation seemed shameful, and he went of his own accord to the town below and began to work, along with other boys of his age, helping to make the mud bricks people used for building their houses.

Living in the town was much as he had imagined it would be. For two years he stayed in a room behind a blacksmith's shop, leading a life without quarrels, and saving whatever money he did not have to spend to keep himself alive. Far from making any friends during this time, he formed a thorough hatred for the people of the town, who never allowed him to forget that he was a son of sin, and therefore not like others, but *meskhot*—damned. Then he found a small house, not much more than a hut, in the palm groves outside the town. The rent was low and no one lived nearby. He went to live there, where the only sound was the wind in the trees, and avoided the people of the town when he could.

One hot summer evening shortly after sunset he was walking under the arcades that faced the town's main square. A few paces ahead of him an old man in a white turban was trying to shift a heavy sack from one shoulder to the other. Suddenly it fell to the ground, and Allal stared as two dark forms flowed out of it and disappeared into the shadows. The old man pounced upon the sack and fastened the top of it, at the same time beginning to shout: Look out for the snakes! Help me find my snakes!

Many people turned quickly around and walked back the way they had come. Others stood at some distance, watching. A few called to the old man: Find your snakes fast and get them out of here! Why are they here? We don't want snakes in this town!

Hopping up and down in his anxiety, the old man turned to Allal. Watch this for me a minute, my son. He pointed at the sack lying on the earth at his feet, and snatching up a basket he had been carrying, went swiftly around the corner into an alley.

Allal stood where he was. No one passed by.

It was not long before the old man returned, panting with triumph. When the onlookers in the square saw him again, they began to call out, this time to Allal: Show that *berrani* the way out of the town! He has no right to carry those things in here. Out! Out!

Allal picked up the big sack and said to the old man: Come on.

They left the square and went through the alleys until they were at the edge of town. The old man looked up then, saw the palm trees black against the fading sky ahead, and turned to the boy beside him.

Come on, said Allal again, and he went to the left along the rough path that led to his house. The old man stood perplexed.

You can stay with me tonight, Allal told him.

And these? he said, pointing first at the sack and then at the basket. They have to be with me.

Allal grinned. They can come.

When they were sitting in the house Allal looked at the sack and the basket. I'm not like the rest of them here, he said.

It made him feel good to hear the words being spoken. He made a contemptuous gesture. Afraid to walk through the square because of a snake. You saw them.

The old man scratched his chin. Snakes are like people, he said. You have to get to know them. Then you can be their friends.

Allal hesitated before he asked: Do you ever let them out?

Always, the old man said with energy. It's bad for them

to be inside like this. They've got to be healthy when they get to Taroudant, or the man there won't buy them.

He began a long story about his life as a hunter of snakes, explaining that each year he made a voyage to Taroudant to see a man who bought them for the Aissaoua snake charmers in Marrakech. Allal made tea while he listened, and brought out a bowl of kif paste to eat with the tea. Later, when they were sitting comfortably in the midst of the pipe smoke, the old man chuckled. Allal turned to look at him.

Shall I let them out?

Fine!

But you must sit and keep quiet. Move the lamp nearer.

He untied the sack, shook it a bit, and returned to where he had been sitting. Then in silence Allal watched the long bodies move cautiously out into the light. Among the cobras were others with markings so delicate and perfect that they seemed to have been designed and painted by an artist. One reddish-gold serpent, which coiled itself lazily in the middle of the floor, he found particularly beautiful. As he stared at it, he felt a great desire to own it and have it always with him.

The old man was talking. I've spent my whole life with snakes, he said. I could tell you some things about them. Did you know that if you give them *majoun* you can make them do what you want, and without saying a word? I swear by Allah!

Allal's face assumed a doubtful air. He did not question the truth of the other's statement, but rather the likelihood of his being able to put the knowledge to use. For it was at that moment that the idea of actually taking the snake first came into his head. He was thinking that whatever he was to do must be done quickly, for the old man would be leaving in the morning. Suddenly he felt a great impatience.

Put them away so I can cook dinner, he whispered. Then he sat admiring the ease with which the old man picked up each one by its head and slipped it into the sack. Once again he dropped two of the snakes into the basket, and one of these, Allal noted, was the red one. He imagined he could see the shining of its scales through the lid of the basket.

As he set to work preparing the meal Allal tried to think of other things. Then, since the snake remained in his mind in spite of everything, he began to devise a way of getting it. While he squatted over the fire in a corner, he mixed some kif paste in a bowl of milk and set it aside.

The old man continued to talk. That was good luck, getting the two snakes back like that, in the middle of the town. You can never be sure what people are going to do when they find out you're carrying snakes. Once in El Kelaa they took all of them and killed them, one after the other, in front of me. A year's work. I had to go back home and start all over again.

Even as they ate, Allal saw that his guest was growing sleepy. How will things happen? he wondered. There was no way of knowing beforehand precisely what he was going to do, and the prospect of having to handle the snake worried him. It could kill me, he thought.

Once they had eaten, drunk tea and smoked a few pipes of kif, the old man lay back on the floor and said he was going to sleep. Allal sprang up. In here! he told him, and led him to his own mat in an alcove. The old man lay down and swiftly fell asleep.

Several times during the next half hour Allal went to the alcove and peered in, but neither the body in its burnoose nor the head in its turban had stirred.

First he got out his blanket, and after tying three of its corners together, spread it on the floor with the fourth corner facing the basket. Then he set the bowl of milk and kif paste on the blanket. As he loosened the strap from the cover of the basket the old man coughed. Allal stood immobile, waiting to hear the cracked voice speak. A small breeze had sprung up, making the palm branches rasp one against the other, but there was no further sound from the alcove. He crept to the far side of the room and squatted by the wall, his gaze fixed on the basket.

Several times he thought he saw the cover move slightly, but each time he decided he had been mistaken. Then he caught his breath. The shadow along the base of the basket was moving. One of the creatures had crept out from the far side. It waited for a while before continuing into the light, but when it did, Allal breathed a prayer of thanks. It was the red and gold one.

When finally it decided to go to the bowl, it made a complete tour around the edge, looking in from all sides, before lowering its head toward the milk. Allal watched, fearful that the foreign flavor of the kif paste might repel it. The snake remained there without moving.

He waited a half hour or more. The snake stayed where it was, its head in the bowl. From time to time, Allal glanced at the basket, to be certain that the second snake was still in it. The breeze went on, rubbing the palm branches together. When he decided it was time, he rose slowly, and keeping an eye on the basket where apparently the other snake still slept, he reached over and gathered together the three tied corners of the blanket. Then he lifted the fourth corner, so that both the snake and the bowl slid in the bottom of the improvised sack. The snake moved slightly, but he did not think it was angry. He knew exactly where he would hide it: between some rocks in the dry riverbed.

Holding the blanket in front of him he opened the door and stepped out under the stars. It was not far up the road, to a group of high palms, and then to the left down into the *oued*. There was a space between the boulders where the bundle would be invisible. He pushed it in with care, and hurried back to the house. The old man was asleep.

There was no way of being sure that the other snake was still in the basket, so Allal picked up his burnoose and went outside. He shut the door and lay down on the ground to sleep.

Before the sun was in the sky the old man was awake, lying in the alcove coughing. Allal jumped up, went inside, and began to make a fire in the *mijmah*. A minute later he heard the other exclaim: They're loose again! Out of the basket! Stay where you are and I'll find them.

It was not long before the old man grunted with satisfaction. I have the black one! he cried. Allal did not look up from the corner where he crouched, and the old man came over, waving a cobra. Now I've got to find the other one.

He put the snake away and continued to search. When the fire was blazing, Allal turned and said: Do you want me to help you look for it?

No, no! Stay where you are.

Allal boiled the water and made the tea, and still the old man was crawling on his knees, lifting boxes and pushing sacks.

His turban had slipped off and his face ran with sweat.

Come and have tea, Allal told him.

The old man did not seem to have heard him at first. Then he rose and went into the alcove, where he rewound his turban. When he came out he sat down with Allal, and they had breakfast.

Snakes are very clever, the old man said. They can get into places that don't exist. I've moved everything in this house.

After they had finished eating, they went outside and looked for the snake between the close-growing trunks of the palms near the house. When the old man was convinced that it was gone, he went sadly back in.

That was a good snake, he said at last. And now I'm going to Taroudant.

They said good-bye, and the old man took his sack and basket and started up the road toward the highway.

All day long as he worked, Allal thought of the snake, but it was not until sunset that he was able to go to the rocks in the *oued* and pull out the blanket. He carried it back to the house in a high state of excitement.

Before he untied the blanket, he filled a wide dish with milk and kif paste, and set it on the floor. He ate three spoonfuls of the paste himself and sat back to watch, drumming on the low wooden tea table with his fingers. Everything happened just as he had hoped. The snake came slowly out of the blanket, and very soon had found the dish and was drinking the milk. As long as it drank he kept drumming; when it had finished and raised its head to look at him, he stopped, and it crawled back inside the blanket.

Later that evening he put down more milk, and drummed again on the table. After a time the snake's head appeared, and finally all of it, and the entire pattern of action was repeated.

That night and every night thereafter, Allal sat with the snake, while with infinite patience he sought to make it his friend. He never attempted to touch it, but soon he was able to summon it, keep it in front of him for as long as he pleased, merely by tapping on the table, and dismiss it at will. For the first week or so he used the kif paste; then he tried the routine without it. In the end the results were the same. After that he fed it only milk and eggs.

Then one evening as his friend lay gracefully coiled in front of him, he began to think of the old man, and formed an idea that put all other things out of his mind. There had not been any kif paste in the house for several weeks, and he decided to make some. He bought the ingredients the following day, and after work he prepared the paste. When it was done, he mixed a large amount of it in a bowl with milk and set it down for the snake. Then he himself ate four spoonfuls, washing them down with tea.

He quickly undressed, and moving the table so that he could reach it, stretched out naked on a mat near the door. This time he continued to tap on the table, even after the snake had finished drinking the milk. It lay still, observing him, as if it were in doubt that the familiar drumming came from the brown body in front of it.

Seeing that even after a long time it remained where it was, staring at him with its stony yellow eyes, Allal began to say to it over and over: Come here. He knew it could not hear his voice, but he believed it could feel his mind as he urged it. You can make them do what you want, without saying a word, the old man had told him.

Although the snake did not move, he went on repeating his command, for by now he knew it was going to come. And after another long wait, all at once it lowered its head and began to move toward him. It reached his hip and slid along his leg. Then it climbed up his leg and lay for a time across his chest. Its body was heavy and tepid, its scales wonderfully smooth. After a time it came to rest, coiled in the space between his head and his shoulder.

By this time the kif paste had completely taken over Allal's mind. He lay in a state of pure delight, feeling the snake's head against his own, without a thought save that he and the snake were together. The patterns forming and melting behind his eyelids seemed to be the same ones that covered the snake's back. Now and then in a huge frenzied movement they all swirled up and shattered into fragments which swiftly became one great yellow eye, split through the middle by the narrow vertical pupil that pulsed with his own heartbeat. Then the eye would recede, through shifting shadow and sunlight, until only the designs of the scales were left, swarming with renewed insistence as they merged and separated. At last the eye returned, so huge this time that it had no edge around it, its pupil dilated to form an aperture almost wide enough for him to enter. As he stared at the blackness within, he understood that he was being slowly propelled toward the opening. He put out his hands to touch the polished surface of the eye on each side, and as he did this he felt the pull from within. He slid through the crack and was swallowed by darkness.

On awakening Allal felt that he had returned from somewhere far away. He opened his eyes and saw, very close to him, what looked like the flank of an enormous beast, covered with coarse stiff hair. There was a repeated vibration in the air, like distant thunder curling around the edges of the sky. He sighed, or imagined that he did, for his breath made no sound. Then he shifted his head a bit, to try and see beyond the mass of hair beside him. Next he saw the ear, and he knew he was looking at his own head from the outside. He had not expected this; he had hoped only that his friend would come in and share his mind with him. But it did not strike him as being at all strange; he merely said to himself that now he was seeing through the eyes of the snake, rather than through his own.

Now he understood why the serpent had been so wary of him: from here the boy was a monstrous creature, with all the bristles on his head and his breathing that vibrated inside him like a far-off storm.

He uncoiled himself and glided across the floor to the alcove. There was a break in the mud wall wide enough to let him out. When he had pushed himself through, he lay full length on the ground in the crystalline moonlight, staring at the strangeness of the landscape, where shadows were not shadows.

He crawled around the side of the house and started up the road toward the town, rejoicing in a sense of freedom different from any he had ever imagined. There was no feeling of having a body, for he was perfectly contained in the skin that covered him. It was beautiful to caress the earth with the length of his belly as he moved along the silent road, smelling the sharp veins of wormwood in the wind. When the voice of the Muezzin floated out over the countryside from the mosque, he could not hear it, or know that within the hour the night would end.

On catching sight of a man ahead, he left the road and hid behind a rock until the danger had passed. But then as he approached the town there began to be more people, so that he let himself down into the *seguia*, the deep ditch that went along beside the road. Here the stones and clumps of dead plants impeded his progress. He was still struggling along the floor of the *seguia* pushing himself around the rocks and through the dry tangles of matted stalks left by the water, when dawn began to break.

The coming of daylight made him anxious and unhappy. He clambered up the bank of the *seguia* and raised his head to examine the road. A man walking past saw him, stood quite still, and then turned and ran back. Allal did not wait; he wanted now to get home as fast as possible.

Once he felt the thud of a stone as it struck the ground somewhere behind him. Quickly he threw himself over the edge of the *seguia* and rolled squirming down the bank. He knew the terrain here: where the road crossed the oued, there were two culverts not far apart. A man stood at some distance ahead of him with a shovel, peering down into the *seguia*. Allal kept moving, aware that he would reach the first culvert before the man could get to him.

The floor of the tunnel under the road was ribbed with hard little waves of sand. The smell of the mountains was in the air that moved through. There were places in here where he could have hidden, but he kept moving, and soon reached the other end. Then he continued to the second culvert and went under the road in the other direction, emerging once again into the *seguia*. Behind him several men had gathered at the entrance to the first culvert. One of them was on his knees, his head and shoulders inside the opening.

He now set out for the house in a straight line across the open ground, keeping his eye on the clump of palms beside it. The sun had just come up, and the stones began to cast long bluish shadows. All at once a small boy appeared from behind some nearby palms, saw him, and opened his eyes and mouth wide with fear. He was so close that Allal went straight to him and bit him in the leg. The boy ran wildly toward the group of men in the *seguia*.

Allal hurried on to the house, looking back only as he reached the hole between the mud bricks. Several men were running among the trees toward him. Swiftly he glided through into the alcove. The brown body still lay near the door. But there was no time, and Allal needed time to get back to it, to lie close to its head and say: Come here.

As he stared out into the room at the body, there was a great pounding on the door. The boy was on his feet at the first blow, as if a spring had been released, and Allal saw with despair the expression of total terror in his face, and the eyes with no mind behind them. The boy stood panting, his fists clenched. The door opened and some of the men peered inside. Then with a roar the boy lowered his head and rushed through the doorway. One of the men reached out to seize him, but lost his balance and fell. An instant later all of them turned and began to run through the palm grove after the naked figure.

Even when, from time to time, they lost sight of him, they could hear the screams, and then they would see him, between the palm trunks, still running. Finally he stumbled and fell face downward. It was then that they caught him, bound him, covered his nakedness, and took him away, to be sent one day soon to the hospital at Berrechid.

That afternoon the same group of men came to the house to carry out the search they had meant to make earlier. Allal lay in the alcove, dozing. When he awoke, they were already inside. He turned and crept to the hole. He saw the man waiting there, a club in his hand.

The rage had always been in his heart; now it burst forth. As if his body were a whip, he sprang into the room. The men nearest him were on their hands and knees, and Allal had the joy of pushing his fangs into two of them before a third severed his head with an axe.

THE QUEST FOR BLANK
CLAVERINGI

Patricia Highsmith

Avery Clavering, a professor of zoology at a California university, heard of the giant snails of Kuwa in a footnote of a book on
molluscs. His sabbatical had been coming up in three months
when he read the few lines:

It is said by Matusas Islands natives that snails even
larger than this exist on the uninhabited island of
Kuwa, twenty-five miles distant from the Matusas. The
Matusans claim that these snails have a shell diameter
of twenty feet and that they are man-eating. Dr. Wm J.
Stead, now living in the Matusas, visited Kuwa in 1949
without finding any snails at all, but the legend persists.

The item aroused Professor Clavering's interest, because he very much wanted to discover some animal, bird, reptile or even mollusc to which he could give his name. *Something-or-other Claveringi.* The professor was forty-eight. His time, perhaps, was not growing short, but he had achieved no particular renown. The discovery of a new species would win him immortality in his field.

The Matusas, the professor saw on a map, were three small islands arranged like the points of an isosceles triangle not far from Hawaii. He wrote a letter to Dr. Stead and received the following reply, written on an abominable typewriter, so many words pale, he could scarcely read it:

April 8th, 19—

Dear Professor Clavering:

I have long heard of the giant snails of Kuwa, but before you make a trip of such length, I must tell you that the natives here assure me a group of them went about twenty years ago to Kuwa to exterminate these so-called man-eating snails which they imagined could swim the ocean between Kuwa and the Matusas and do some damage to the latter island. They claim to have killed off the whole community of them except for one old fellow they could not kill. This is typical of native stories—there's always one that got away. I haven't much doubt the snails were not bigger than three feet across and that they were not **** (here a word was illegible, due both to the pale ribbon and a squashed insect). You say you read of my effort in 1949 to find the giant snails. What the footnote did not say is that I have made several trips since to find them. I retired to the Matusas, in fact, for that purpose. I now believe the snails to be mere folklore, a figment of the natives' imagination. If I were you, I would not waste time or money on an expedition.

Yours sincerely,
Wm J. Stead, M.D.

Professor Clavering had the money and the time. He detected a sourness in Dr. Stead's letter. Maybe Dr. Stead had just had bad luck. By post, Professor Clavering hired a thirty-foot sail-boat with an auxiliary motor from Hawaii. He wanted to make the trip alone from the Matusas. *Blank Claveringi*. Regardless of the size, the snail was apt to be different from any known snail, because of its isolation—if it existed. He planned to go one month ahead of his wife and to join her and their twenty-year-old daughter Wanda in Hawaii for a more orthodox holiday after he had visited Kuwa. A month would give him plenty of time to find the snail, even if there were only one, to take photographs, and make notes.

It was late June when Professor Clavering, equipped with water tanks, tinned beef, soup and milk, biscuits, writing materials, camera, knife, hatchet and a Winchester .22 which he hardly knew how to use, set forth from one of the Matusas bound for Kuwa. Dr. Stead, who had been his host for a few days, saw him off. Dr. Stead was seventy-five, he said, but he looked older, due perhaps to the ravages of drink and the apparently aimless life he led now. He had not looked for the giant snail in two years, he said.

"I've given the last third of my life to looking for this snail, you might say," Dr. Stead added. "But that's man's fate, I suppose, the pursuit of the non-existent. Well—good luck to you, Professor Clavering!" He waved his old American straw hat as the *Samantha* left the dock under motor power.

Professor Clavering had made out to Stead that if he did find snails, he would come back at once, get some natives to accompany him, and return to Kuwa with materials to make crates for the snails. Stead had expressed doubt whether he could persuade any natives to accompany him, if the snail or snails were really large. But then, Dr. Stead had been negative about everything pertaining to Professor Clavering's quest. Professor Clavering was glad to get away from him.

After about an hour, Professor Clavering cut the motor and tentatively hoisted some sail. The wind was favourable, but he knew little about sails, and he paid close attention to his compass. At last, Kuwa came into view, a tan hump on a sea of blue. He was quite close before he saw any greenery, and this was only the tops of some trees. Already, he was looking for anything resembling a giant snail, and regretting he had not brought binoculars, but the island was only three miles long and one mile broad. He decided to aim for a small beach. He dropped anchor, two of them, in water so clear he could see the sand under it. He stood for a few minutes on the deck.

The only life he saw was a few birds in the tops of trees, brightly coloured, crested birds, making cries he had never heard before. There was no low-lying vegetation whatsoever, none of the grass and reeds that might have been expected on an island such as this—much like the Matusas in the soil colour—and this augured well of the presence of snails that might have devoured everything green within their reach. It was only a quarter to two. Professor Clavering ate part of a papaya, two boiled eggs, and brewed coffee on his alcohol burner, as he had had nothing to eat since 6 A.M. Then with his hunting knife and hatchet in the belt of his khaki shorts, and his camera around his neck, he lowered himself into the water. The *Samantha* carried no rowboat.

He sank up to his neck, but he could walk on the bottom. He held the camera high. He emerged panting, as he was some twenty pounds overweight. Professor Clavering was to regret every one of those pounds before the day was over, but as he got his breath and looked around him, and felt himself drying off in the warm sunlight, he was happy. He wiped his hatchet and knife with dry sand, then walked inland, alert for the rounded form of a snail's shell, moving or stationary, anywhere. But as snails were more or less nocturnal, he thought any snails might well be sleeping in some cave or crevice with no idea of emerging until nightfall.

He decided to cross the island first, then follow the coast to right or left and circle the island. He had not gone a quarter of a mile, when his heart gave a leap. Ten yards before him, he saw three bent saplings with their top leaves chewed off. The young trees were four inches in diameter at their base. It would have taken a considerable weight to bend them down, something like a hundred pounds. The professor looked on the trees and the ground for the glaze left by snails, but found none. But rain could have washed it away. A snail whose shell was three feet in diameter would not weigh enough to bend such a tree, so Professor Clavering now hoped for something bigger. He pushed on.

He arrived at the other side of the island. The sea had eaten a notch into the shore, forming a mostly dry gully of a hundred yards' length and a depth of thirty feet. The land here was sandy but moist, and there was, he saw, a little vegetation in the form of patchy grass. But here, the lower branches of all the trees had been divested of their leaves, and so long ago that the branches had dried and fallen off. All this bespoke the presence of land snails. Professor Clavering stooped and looked down into the gulley. He saw, just over the edge of his side of the crevice, the pink-tan curve of something that was neither rock nor sand. If it was a snail, it was monstrous. Involuntarily, he took a step backward, scattering pebbles down the gulley.

The professor ran round the gulley to have a better look. It was a snail, and its shell was about fifteen feet high. He had a view of its left side, the side without the spiral. It resembled a peach-coloured sail filled with wind, and the sunlight made nacreous, silvery patches gleam and twinkle as the great thing stirred. The little rain of pebbles had aroused it, the professor realized. If the shell was fifteen or eighteen feet in diameter, he reckoned that the snail's body or foot would be something like six yards long when extended. Rooted to the spot, the professor stood, thrilled as much by the (as yet) empty phrase *Blank Claveringi* which throbbed in his head as by the fact he was looking upon something no man had seen before, or at least no scientist. The crate would have to be bigger than he had thought, but the *Samantha* would be capable of taking it on her forward deck.

The snail was backing to pull its head from the narrow part of the gulley. The moist body, the color of tea with milk, came into view with the slowness of an enormous snake awakening from slumber. All was silent, except for pebbles dropping from the snail's underside as it lifted its head, except for the professor's constrained breathing. The snail's head, facing inland, rose higher and higher, and its antennae, with which it saw, began to extend. Professor Clavering realized he had disturbed it from its diurnal sleep, and a brief terror caused him to retreat again, sending more pebbles down the slope.

The snail heard this, and slowly turned its enormous head toward him.

The professor felt paralysed. A gigantic face regarded him, a face with drooping, scalloped cheeks or lips, with antennae six feet long now, the eyes on the ends of them scrutinizing him at his own level and scarcely ten feet away, with the disdain of a Herculean lorgnette, with the unknown potency of a pair of oversized telescopes. The snail reared so high, it had to arch its antennae to keep him in view. Six yards long? It would be more like eight or ten yards. The snail turned itself to move toward him.

Still, the professor did not budge. He knew about snails' teeth, the twenty-odd thousand pairs of them even in a small garden snail, set in comblike structures, the upper front teeth visible, moving up and down constantly just under transparent flesh. A snail of this size, with proportionate teeth, could chew through a tree as quickly as a woodsman's axe, the professor thought. The snail was advancing up the bank with monumental confidence. He had to stand still for a few seconds simply to admire it. *His* snail! The professor opened his camera and took a picture, just as the snail was hauling its shell over the edge of the quarry.

"You are magnificent!" Professor Clavering said in a soft and awestruck voice. Then he took a few steps backward.

It was pleasant to think he could skip nimbly about, comparatively speaking, observing the snail from all angles, while the snail could only creep toward him at what seemed the rate of one yard in ten seconds. The professor thought to watch the snail for an hour or so, then go back to the *Samantha* and write some notes. He would sleep aboard the boat, take some more photographs tomorrow morning, then start under engine power back to the Matusas. He trotted for twenty yards, then turned to watch the snail approach.

The snail travelled with its head lifted three feet above the ground, keeping the professor in the focus of its eyes. It was moving faster. Professor Clavering retreated sooner than he intended, and before he could get another picture.

Now Professor Clavering looked around for a mate of the snail. He was rather glad not to see another snail, but he cautioned himself not to rule out the possibility of a mate. It wouldn't be pleasant to be cornered by two snails, yet the idea excited him. Impossible to think of a situation in which he could not escape from two slow, lumbering creatures like the—the what? *Amygdalus Persica* (his mind stuck on peaches, because of the beautiful colour of the shell) *Carnivora* (perhaps) *Claveringi*. That could be improved upon, the professor thought as he walked backward, watching.

A little grove of trees gave him an idea. If he stood in the grove, the snail could not reach him, and he would also have a close view. The professor took a stand amid twelve or fifteen trees, all about twenty feet high. The snail did not slacken its speed, but began to circle the grove, still watching the professor. Finding no opening big enough between two trees, the snail raised its head higher, fifteen feet high, and began to creep up on the trees. Branches cracked, and one tree snapped.

Professor Clavering ducked and retreated. He had a glimpse of a great belly gliding unhurt over a jagged tree trunk, of a circular mouth two feet across, opening and showing the still wider upper band of teeth like shark's teeth, munching automatically up and down. The snail cruised gently down over the tree tops, some of which sprang back into position as the snail's weight left them.

Click! went the professor's camera.

What a sight that had been! Something like a slow hurdle. He imagined entertaining friends with an account of it, substantiated by the photograph, once he got back to California. Old Professor McIlroy of the biology department had laughed at him for spending seven thousand dollars on an effort he predicted would be futile!

Professor Clavering was tiring, so he cut directly for the *Samantha*. He noticed that the snail veered also in a direction that would intercept him, if they kept on at their steady though different speeds, and the professor chuckled and trotted for a bit. The snail also picked up speed, and the professor remembered the wide, upward rippling of the snail's body as it had hurdled the trees. It would be interesting to see how fast the snail could go on a straight course. Such a test would have to wait for America.

He reached the water and saw his beach a few yards away to his right, but no ship was there. He'd made a mistake, he thought, and his beach was on the other side of the island. Then he caught sight of the *Samantha* half a mile out on the ocean, drifting away.

"*Damn!*" Professor Clavering said aloud. He'd done something wrong with the anchors. Did he dare try to swim to it? The distance frightened him, and it was growing wider every moment.

A rattle of pebbles behind him made him turn. The snail was hardly twenty feet away.

The Professor trotted down toward the beach. There was bound to be some slit on the coast, a cave however small, where he could be out of reach of the snail. He wanted to rest for a while. What really annoyed him now was the prospect of a chilly night without blankets or food. The Matusas natives had been right: there was nothing to eat on Kuwa.

Professor Clavering stopped dead, his shoes sliding on sand and pebbles. Before him, not fifty feet away on the beach, was another snail as big as the one following him, and somewhat lighter in colour. Its tail was in the sea, and its muzzle dripped water as it reared itself to get a look at him.

It was this snail, the professor realized, that had chewed through the hemp ropes and let the boat go free. Was there something about new hemp ropes that appealed to snails? This question he put out of his mind for the nonce. He had a snail before and behind him. The professor trotted on along the shore. The only crevice of shelter he was sure existed was the gulley on the other side of the island. He forced himself to walk at a moderate pace for a while, to breathe normally, then he sat down and treated himself to a rest.

The first snail was the first to appear, and as it had lost sight of him, it lifted its head and looked slowly to right and left, though without slackening its progress. The professor sat motionless, bare head lowered, hoping the snail would not see him. But he was not that lucky. The snail saw him and altered course to a straight line for him. Behind it came the second snail—it's wife? its husband?—the professor could not tell and there was no way of telling.

Professor Clavering had to leave his resting place. The weight of his hatchet reminded him that he at least had a weapon. A good scare, he thought, a minor wound might discourage them. He knew they were hungry, that their teeth could tear his flesh more easily than they tore trees, and that alive or dead, he would be eaten by these snails if he permitted it to happen. He drew his hatchet and faced them, conscious that he cut a not very formidable figure with his slight paunch, his pale, skinny legs, his height of five feet seven, about a third the snails' height, but his brows above his glasses were set with a determination to defend his life.

The first snail reared when it was ten feet away. The professor advanced and swung the hatchet at the projecting mantle on the snail's left side. He had not dared get close enough, his aim was inches short, and the weight of the hatchet pulled the professor off balance. He staggered and fell under the raised muzzle, and had just time to roll himself from under the descending mouth before it touched the ground where he had been. Angry now, he circled the snail and swung a blow at the nacreous shell, which turned the blade. The hatchet took an inch-deep chip, but nothing more. The professor swung again, higher this time and in the centre of the shell's posterior, trying for the lung valve beneath, but the valve was still higher, he knew, ten feet from the ground, and once more his hatchet took only a chip. The snail began to turn itself to face him.

The professor then confronted the second snail, rushed at it and swung the hatchet, cutting it in the cheek. The hatchet sank up to its wooden handle, and he had to tug to get it out, and then had to run a few yards, as the snail put on speed and reared its head for a biting attack. Glancing back, the professor saw that no liquid (he had not, of course, expected blood) came from the cut in the snail's cheek, and in fact he couldn't see the cut. And the blow had certainly been no discouragement to the snail's advance.

Professor Clavering began to walk at a sensible pace straight for the snails' lair on the other side of the island. By the time he scrambled down the side of the gulley, he was winded and his legs hurt. But he saw to his relief that the gulley narrowed to a sharp V. Wedged in that, he would be safe. Professor Clavering started into the V, which had an overhanging top rather like a cave, when he saw that what he had taken for some rounded rocks were moving—at least some of them were. They were baby snails! They were larger than good-sized beach balls. And the professor saw, from the way a couple of them were devouring grass blades, that they were hungry.

A snail's head appeared high on his left. The giant parent snail began to descend the gulley. A crepitation, a pair of antennae against the sky on his right, heralded the arrival of the second snail. He had nowhere to turn except the sea, which was not a bad idea, he thought, as these were land snails. The professor waded out and turned left, walking waist-deep in water. It was slow going, and a snail was coming after him. He got closer to the land and ran in thigh-deep water.

The first snail, the darker one, entered the water boldly and crept along in a depth of several inches, showing signs of being willing to go into deeper water when it got abreast of Professor Clavering. The professor hoped the other snail, maybe the mother, had stayed with the young. But it hadn't. It was following along the land, and accelerating. The professor plunged wildly for the shore where he would be able to move faster.

Now, thank goodness, he saw rocks. Great igneous masses of rocks covered a sloping hill down to the sea. There was bound to be a niche, some place there where he could take shelter. The sun was sinking into the ocean, it would be dark soon, and there was no moon, he knew. The professor was thirsty. When he reached the rocks, he flung himself like a corpse into a trough made by four or five scratchy boulders, which caused him to lie in a curve. The rocks rose two feet above his body, and the trough was hardly a foot wide. A snail couldn't, he reasoned, stick its head down there and bite him.

The peachy curves of the snails' shells appeared, and one, the second, drew closer.

"I'll strike it with my hatchet if it comes!" the professor swore to himself. "I'll cut its face to ribbons with my knife!" He was now reconciled to killing both adults, because he could take back a pair of the young ones, and in fact more easily because they were smaller.

The snail seemed to sniff like a dog, though inaudibly as its muzzle hovered over the professor's hiding place. Then with majestic calm it came down on the rocks between which the professor lay. Its slimy foot covered the aperture and within seconds had blocked out almost all the light.

Professor Clavering drew his hunting knife in anger and panic, and plunged it several times into the snail's soft flesh. The snail seemed not even to wince. A few seconds later, it stopped moving, though the professor knew that it was not only not dead, as the stabs hadn't touched any vital organ, but that it had fastened itself over his trench in the firmest possible way. No slit of light showed. The professor was only grateful that the irregularity of the rocks must afford a supply of air. Now he pressed frantically with his palms against the snail's body, and felt his hands slip and scrape against rock. The firmness of the snail, his inability to budge it, made him feel slightly sick for a moment.

An hour passed. The professor almost slept, but the experience was more like a prolonged hallucination. He dreamed, or feared, that he was being chewed by twenty thousand pairs of teeth into a heap of mince, which the two giant snails shared with their offspring. To add to his misery, he was cold and hungry. The snail's body gave no warmth, and was even cool.

Some hours later, the professor awoke and saw stars above him. The snail had departed. It was pitch dark. He stood up cautiously, trying not to make a sound, and stepped out of the crevice. He was free! On a sandy stretch of beach a few yards away, Professor Clavering lay down, pressed against a vertical face of rock. Here he slept the remaining hours until dawn.

He awakened just in time, and perhaps not the dawn but

a sixth sense had awakened him. The first snail was coming toward him and was only ten feet away. The professor got up on trembling legs, and trotted inland, up a slope. An idea came to him: if he could push a boulder of, say, five hundred pounds— possible with a lever—on to an adult snail in the gulley, and smash the spot below which its lung lay, then he could kill it. Otherwise, he could think of no other means at his disposal that could inflict a fatal injury. His gun might, but the gun was on the *Samantha*. He had already estimated that it might be a week, or never, that help would come from the Matusas. The *Samantha* would not necessarily float back to the Matusas, would not necessarily be seen by any other ship for days, and even if it was seen, would it be apparent she was drifting? And if so, would the spotters make a beeline for the Matusas to report it? Not necessarily. The professor bent quickly and licked some dew from a leaf. The snails were twenty yards behind him now.

The trouble is, I'm becoming exhausted, he said to himself.

He was even more tired at noon. Only one snail pursued him, but the professor imagined the other resting or eating a tree top, in order to be fresh later. The professor could trot a hundred yards, find a spot to rest in, but he dared not shut his eyes for long, lest he sleep. And he was definitely weak from lack of food.

So the day passed. His idea of dropping a rock down the gulley was thwarted by two factors: the second snail was guarding the gulley now, at the top of its V, and there was no such rock as he needed within a hundred yards.

When dusk came, the professor could not find the hill where the igneous rocks were. Both snails had him in their sight now. His watch said a quarter to seven. Professor Clavering took a deep breath and faced the fact that he must make an attempt to kill one or both snails before dark. Almost without thinking, or planning—he was too spent for that—he chopped down a slender tree and hacked off its branches. The leaves of these branches were devoured by the two snails five minutes after the branches had fallen to the ground. The professor dragged his tree several yards inland, and sharpened one end of it with the hatchet. It was too heavy a weapon for one hand to wield, but in two hands, it made a kind of battering ram, or giant spear.

At once, Professor Clavering turned and attacked, running with the spear pointed slightly upward. He aimed for the first snail's mouth, but struck too low, and the tree end penetrated about four inches into the snail's chest—or the area below its face. No vital organ here, except the long, straight oesophagus, which in these giant snails would be set deeper than four inches. He had nothing for his trouble but lacerated hands. His spear hung for a few seconds in the snail's flesh, then fell out on to the ground. The professor retreated, pulling his hatchet from his belt. The second snail, coming up abreast of the other, paused to chew off a few inches of the tree stump, then joined its mate in giving attention to Professor Clavering. There was something contemptuous, something absolutely assured, about the snails' slow progress toward him, as if they were thinking, "Escape us a hundred, a thousand times, we shall finally reach you and devour every trace of you."

The professor advanced once more, circled the snail he had just hit with the tree spear, and swung his hatchet at the rear of its shell. Desperately, he attacked the same spot with five or six direct hits, for now he had a plan. His hacking operation had to be halted, because the second snail was coming up behind him. Its snout and an antenna even brushed the professor's legs moistly and staggered him, before he could step out of its way. Two more hatchet blows the professor got in, and then he stopped, because his right arm hurt. He had by no means gone through the shell, but he had no strength for more effort with the hatchet. He went back for his spear. His target was a small one, but he ran toward it with desperate purpose.

The blow landed. It even broke through.

The professor's hands were further torn, but he was oblivious of them. His success made him as joyous as if he had killed both his enemies, as if a rescue ship with food, water, and a bed were even then sailing into Kuwa's beach.

The snail was twisting and rearing up with pain.

Professor Clavering ran forward, lifted the drooping spear and pushed it with all his might farther into the snail, pointing it upward to go as close as possible to the lung. Whether the snail died soon or not, it was *hors de combat,* the professor saw. And he himself experienced something like physical collapse an instant after seeing the snail's condition. He was quite incapable of taking on the other snail in the same manner, and the other snail was coming after him. The professor tried to walk in a straight line away from both snails, but he weaved with fatigue and faintness. He looked behind him. The unhurt snail was thirty feet away. The wounded snail faced him, but was motionless, half in and half out of its shell, suffering in silence some agony of asphyxiation. Professor Clavering walked on.

Quite by accident, just as it was growing dark, he came

upon his field of rocks. Among them he took shelter for the second time. The snail's snout probed the trench in which he lay, but he could not quite reach him. Would it not be better to remain in the trench tomorrow, to hope for rain for water? He fell asleep before he could come to any decision.

Again, when the professor awakened at dawn, the snail had departed. His hands throbbed. Their palms were encrusted with dried blood and sand. He thought it wise to go to the sea and wash them in salt water.

The giant snail lay between him and the sea, and at his approach, the snail very slowly began to creep toward him. Professor Clavering made a wobbling detour and continued on his way toward the water. He dipped his hands and moved them rapidly back and forth, at last lifted water to his face, longed to wet his dry mouth, warned himself that he should not, and yielded anyway, spitting out the water almost at once. Land snails hated salt and could be killed by salt crystals. The professor angrily flung handfuls of water at the snail's face. The snail only lifted its head higher, out of the professor's range. Its form was slender now, and it had, oddly, the grace of a horned gazelle, of some animal of the deer family. The snail lowered its snout, and the professor trudged away, but not quickly enough: the snail came down on his shoulder and the suctorial mouth clamped.

The professor screamed. *My God,* he thought, as a piece of his shirt, a piece of flesh and possibly bone was torn from his left shoulder, *why was I such an ass as to linger?* The snail's weight pushed him under, but it was shallow here, and he struggled to his feet and walked toward the land. Blood streamed hotly down his side. He could not bear to look at his shoulder to see what had happened, and would not have been surprised if his left arm had dropped off in the next instant. The professor walked on aimlessly in shallow water near the land. He was still going faster than the snail.

Then he lifted his eyes to the empty horizon, and saw a dark spot in the water in the mid-distance. He stopped, wondering if it were real or a trick of his eyes: but now he made out the double body of a catamaran, and he thought he saw Dr. Stead's straw hat. They had come from the Matusas!

"Hello!" the professor was shocked at the hoarseness, the feebleness of his voice. Not a chance that he had been heard.

But with hope now, the professor's strength increased. He headed for a little beach—not his beach, a smaller one—and when he got there he stood in its centre, his good arm raised, and shouted, "Dr. *Stead!* This way!—On the beach!" He could definitely see Dr. Stead's hat and four dark heads.

There was no answering shout. Professor Clavering could not tell if they had heard him or not. And the accursed snail was only thirty feet away now! He'd lost his hatchet, he realized. And the camera that had been under water with him was now ruined, and so were the two pictures in it. No matter. He would live.

"*Here!*" he shouted, again lifting his arm.

The natives heard this. Suddenly all heads in the catamaran turned to him.

Dr. Stead pointed to him and gesticulated, and dimly Professor Clavering heard the good doctor urging the boatman to make for the shore. He saw Dr. Stead half stand up in the catamaran.

The natives gave a whoop—at first Professor Clavering thought it a whoop of joy, or of recognition, but almost at once a wild swing of the sail, a splash of a couple of oars, told him that the natives were trying to change their course.

Pebbles crackled. The snail was near. And this of course was what the natives had seen—the giant snail.

"Please—Here!" the professor screamed. He plunged again into the water. *"Please!"*

Dr. Stead was trying, that the professor could see. But the natives were rowing, paddling with hands even, and their sail was carrying them obliquely away.

The snail made a splash as it entered the sea. To drown or to be eaten alive? The professor wondered. He was waist-deep when he stumbled, waist-deep but head under when the snail crashed down upon him, and he realized as the thousands of pairs of teeth began to gnaw at his back, that his fate was both to drown and to be chewed to death.

BIOGRAPHIES

Paul Bowles, *born in New York City in 1911, studied music under Aaron Copeland and lived his later years in Morocco with his wife, the author Jane Bowles. Tangier was the setting of Bowles's most famous novel,* The Sheltering Sky. *Writing in a serious, almost detached style, he often recounted the experiences of Westerners caught up in bewildering circumstances in cultures about which they understood little. Westerners reading Bowles's story in this collection, "Allal," will find themselves embraced by the life of a boy in an utterly foreign culture, whose deepest fears and desires are not too different than their own.*

Patricia Highsmith *was born in Texas in 1921 and spent the latter half of her life in Europe, writing and painting. She is best known today for her novel* The Talented Mr. Ripley *and for a series of suspense novels that includes* Strangers on a Train *and* The Glass Cell. *Of her many terror stories, "The Quest for Blank Claveringi" is one of the few in which the animal is the least-appealing character.*

Edward D. Hoch *has written literally hundreds of short stories, including a series about a thief who steals things no one much wants. His horror stories date back to the 1960s, many published in* The Magazine of Horror.

Nancy Holder *is the author of 60 novels and more than 200 short stories. As a child she gave her Barbie dolls Viking burials in her* backyard, and she is now the mother of a young daughter. She has been awarded four Bram Stoker Awards for Outstanding Achievement from the Horror Writers Association.

Graham Joyce *is the author of "Xenos Beach," a modern ghost story in which a young Brit, wandering in Greece, is induced to swim in a deadly current by a siren who looks only too real. The idea for the story occurred to Joyce when he was staying on the Greek island of Chios. Coming upon empty tents bleaching in the sun, he couldn't help wondering to whom they had belonged and why they'd been abandoned.*

Joyce has been four times the winner of the British Fantasy Society's August Derleth Award. His novels include Dark Sister *(1992),* Requiem *(1995),* The Tooth Fairy *(1996), and* Indigo *(1999).*

Joe R. Lansdale *enjoys spinning "over-the-top" yarns of horror and suspense, especially those about the American West. A resident of Nacagdoches, Texas, Lansdale's standard workday is six hours at the typewriter followed by three hours teaching in his martial-arts studio. The author of more than 20 books, Lansdale has received five Bram Stoker Awards. A* New York Times *book review described the author as having "a folklorist's eye for telling detail and a front-porch raconteur's sense of pace."*

Jerry MacDonald *was a Canadian writer who wrote several stories for* Reader's Digest.

Michael Norman, *long interested in the haunted places of America, has traveled throughout the country tracking down stories of ghosts and haunted places. Presently, he teaches in the* *journalism department at the University of Wisconsin–River Falls and lives in River Falls. His collaborator,* **Beth Scott,** *who died in early 1994, was a full-time freelance writer for over 35 years. Scott and Norman authored* Haunted America *and* Historic Haunted America. *Norman's most recent book is* Haunted Heritage.

Talmage Powell, *a versatile, skillful Southern writer born in 1920, wrote suspense, action, and horror stories under his own name and under numerous pseudonyms. His more than 500 short stories include this anthology's "Survival Exercise," which combines all of his best elements: suspense, action, and horror. Mr. Powell's best-known novels center around a realistically described Tampa, Florida, private detective named Ed Rivers. These include* The Killer Is Mine, Start Screaming Murder, *and* The Girl's Number Doesn't Answer.

David Poyer *left his native Western Pennsylvania for the Navy at 17. Although the bulk of his writing since has consisted of sea fiction, Poyer also set four hauntingly crafted novels in remote, mysterious "Hemlock County," Pennsylvania. The prologue to the third,* As the Wolf Loves Winter, *is included in this anthology.*

Alan Ryan *is a novelist and journalist and winner of the World Fantasy Award and the Lowell Thomas Travel Journalism Award. He lives in Rio de Janeiro, Brazil, and writes frequently for the* Washington Post *and the* Cleveland Plain Dealer.

William Sambrot, *who also wrote under the pseudonyms Anthony Ayes and William Ayes, has been a prolific magazine writer whose stories have appeared in* Cosmopolitan, Playboy, *and the*

Saturday Evening Post. *His best-known collection of short stories,* Island of Fear and Other Stories, *was published in 1963.*

David B. Silva *has written five novels, his most recent (the first of a trilogy) written with Kevin McCarthy and called* The Family, Book One: Special Effects. *His novel* Legacy, *an account of epic horror, spans over 40 years, as Aaron Hawke leaves the innocence of childhood behind to fight a recurring evil. Silva's short fiction has appeared in* The Year's Best Horror, The Year's Best Fantasy & Horror, *and* The Best American Mystery Stories. *In 1991 he won a Bram Stoker Award for this short story "The Calling."*

Will Smith and R. J. Robbins *collaborated on at least three memorable stories. They are "Swamp Horror," published in the classic horror magazine* Weird Tales *in 1926, as well as the stories "Under the N-Ray" (1925) and "The Soul Master" (1930).*

H. G. Wells, *novelist, historian, journalist, and sociologist, was born into a lower-middle-class British family in 1866. As a young man he studied science in London with the well-known biologist Thomas Huxley, and it was scientific discoveries and their possibilities that inspired his imagination and became the focal point of his famous science-fiction fantasy novels. These include* The Time Machine *(1895),* The Invisible Man *(1897), and* War of the Worlds *(1898). A political progressive and an agitator for liberal causes, Wells grew increasingly pessimistic about the human condition in the wake of World War I. One of his last books,* The Shape of Things to Come *(1933), warned against fascism. Herbert George Wells died in 1946.*

ACKNOWLEDGMENTS

"Ice Sculptures" by David B. Silva. Copyright © 1988 by David B. Silva. Reprinted with permission of author. "Creature of the Snows" by William Sambrot. Copyright © 1960 by William Sambrot. First appeared in the *Saturday Evening Post*. Now appears in *Island of Fear and Other Fiction Stories*, Pocketbooks, 1963. Reprinted by permission of Curtis Brown, Ltd. "Xenos Beach" by Graham Joyce. Copyright © 2000 by Graham Joyce. Published by permission of Graham Joyce c/o Ralph M. Vicinanza, Ltd. "Death to the Easter Bunny" by Alan Ryan. Copyright © 1983 by Alan Ryan. Reprinted by permission of Ellen Levine Literary Agency. "We Have Always Lived in the Forest" by Nancy L. Holder. Copyright © 1987 by Nancy L. Holder. From *Shadows* by Nancy L. Holder. Reprinted by permission of the author. Prologue from *As the Wolf Loves Winter* by David Poyer. Copyright © 1996 by David Poyer. Reprinted by permission of David Poyer and ICM. "Caught in the Jaws of Death" by Jerry MacDonald. Reprinted with permission from the January 1995 *Reader's Digest*. Copyright © 1995 by The Reader's Digest Assn., Inc. "Survival Exercise" by Talmage Powell. Copyright © 1981 by Talmage Powell. Reprinted by permission of Paul Powell. "Swamp Horror" by Will Smith and R. J. Robbins. Copyright © 1927 by Weird Tales, Ltd. Reprinted by permission of Victor Dricks. "Waziah" by Joe R. Lansdale. Copyright © 1981 by Joe R. Lansdale. Reprinted by permission of The Vines Agency, Inc., New York, N.Y. "Bloody Polly" by Michael Norman and Beth Scott as taken from *Haunted America*. Copyright © 1994 Michael Norman and Beth Scott. Reprinted by permission of the authors. "The Faceless Thing" by Edward D. Hoch. Copyright © 1963 by Edward D. Hoch. Reprinted by permission of author. "Allal" by Paul Bowles. As taken from *A Distant Episode: The Selected Stories* by Paul Bowles. Copyright © 1988 by Paul Bowles. Reprinted by permission of HarperCollins Publishers Inc. "The Quest for Blank Claveringi" by Patricia Highsmith. Copyright © 1967, 1970 by Patricia Highsmith. From *Eleven* by Patricia Highsmith. Used by permission of Grove/Atlantic.